ROSS MACDONALD

Find a Victim

Vintage Crime/Black Lizard

Vintage Books

A Division of Random House, Inc.

New York

FIRST VINTAGE CRIME/BLACK LIZARD EDITION,
AUGUST 2001

The Library of Congress has cataloged the Knopf edition as
follows:
Macdonald, John Ross.
Find a victim [by] John Ross Macdonald [pseud.]
New York, Knopf, 1954.
p. cm.
PZ3.M59942 Fi
1381659
CIP

Vintage ISBN: 0-375-70867-7

www.vintagebooks.com

Printed in the United States of America
10 9 8 7 6 5 4 3

To Ivan von Auw, Jr.

A man feared that he might find an assassin;

Another that he might find a victim.

One was more wise than the other.

STEPHEN CRANE

Find a Victim

CHAPTER 1: *He was the ghastliest hitchhiker who* ever thumbed me. He rose on his knees in the ditch. His eyes were black holes in his yellow face, his mouth a bright smear of red like a clown's painted grin. The arm he raised overbalanced him. He fell forward on his face again.

I stamped the brake-pedal and backed a hundred yards to where he lay, a dark-headed man in jeans and a gray workshirt, prone among the jimson. He was as still as death now. But when I squatted down beside him I could hear the sigh and gurgle of his breathing.

Supporting his hip on my knee and his loose head with my arm, I turned him onto his back. The blood at his mouth was breaking in tiny bubbles. The breast of his gray shirt was dark and wet. Unbuttoning it, I saw the round hole among the sodden hairs on his chest, still pumping little bright spurts.

I removed my jacket and tore off my own shirt. Wadding it over the bullet hole, I fixed it in place with my tie. The wounded man stirred and sighed. The eyelids quivered over the dusty-black eyes. He was a young man, and he was dying.

I looked back to the south and then to the north. No cars, no houses, no anything. I had passed one clot of traffic somewhere north of Bakersfield and failed to catch another. It was one of those lulls in time when you can hear your heart ticking your life away, and nothing else. The sun had fallen behind the coastal range, and the valley was filling with twilight. A flight of blackbirds crossed the sky like visible wind, blowing and whiplashing.

3

I lifted him, his head lolling on my chest, and carried him to the car. He was hard to handle, neither big nor heavy but terribly lax. I got him onto the back seat with his head propped up on my overnight bag so that he wouldn't smother, and covered him with the car blanket.

He rode six or seven miles in that position. I turned down my rear-view mirror to keep an eye on him. As the twilight faded, his face in the mirror faded almost out.

I passed a sign: CAMP FREMONT, U.S. MARINE CORPS BASE. Cyclone fence sprang up along the highway. Beyond it streets of weathered barracks marched across the valley to the humpbacked horizon. There wasn't a trace of life. The Quonset hangars of the attached airbase could have been barrows built by a lost race of giants.

Then there were lights at the roadside, a city of lights beyond them. Neons stained the thickening air green and yellow: KERRIGAN'S COURT—DELUXE MOTOR HOTEL. Its lobby and pueblos were brilliantly floodlit. I stopped in front of the lobby and went inside.

It was all blond plywood and green imitation leather furniture. The woman behind the registration desk was also blonde. Her long blue eyes surveyed me, making me conscious of my naked chest. I buttoned my jacket as I crossed the room.

"Can I help you?" she said in a distant way.

"A man in my car needs help, badly. I'll bring him in while you call a doctor."

Her eyebrows moved downward, a worried cleft between them. "Is he sick?"

"With lead poisoning. He's been shot."

She rose in nervous haste and opened a door behind her. "Don, come here a minute."

"He needs a doctor now," I said. "There's no time to talk it over."

"Talk what over?" A big man filled the doorway. He was

heavy-shouldered in a light gabardine suit, and he moved like an ex-athlete gone to seed. "What in hell is it now? Can't you handle anything by yourself?"

Her slim hands wrenched at each other. "I won't permit you to speak to me that way."

He smiled at her without showing his teeth. Under clipped sandy hair, his face was fiery with alcohol or anger. "I talk the way I want to in my own place."

"You're tight, Don."

"You've never seen me tight."

They were standing close to each other in the space behind the desk, face to face in furious intimacy.

I said: "There's a man bleeding to death outside. If you won't let him come in here, at least you can call an ambulance."

He turned to me, his eyes gray triangles under folded lids. "Bleeding to death? Who is he?"

"I don't know. Are you going to get some help for him or not?"

"Yes, of course," the woman said.

She lifted a telephone book out of the desk, found a number, and dialed. The man went out, slamming the door behind him.

"Kerrigan's Motor Court," she said, "Mrs. Kerrigan speaking. We have an injured man here.—No. They say he's been shot.—Yes, it seems to be serious, an emergency."

She replaced the receiver. "The county hospital is sending an ambulance." She added in a low voice, hardly more than a whisper: "I'm sorry for what happened. In our family we don't rise to an emergency. We sink beneath it."

"It doesn't matter."

"It does to me. I'm *really* sorry."

Her face slanted forward across the desk. Her pale smooth hair was drawn back severely from it, as if to emphasize its stark beauty.

"Isn't there anything else I can do?" she said on a rising note. "Call the police?"

"The hospital will. They're required to by law. Thanks for your trouble, Mrs. Kerrigan."

She followed me to the door, a troubled woman who had missed her chance to react like a human being and couldn't let it go. "This must be a terrible thing for you. Is he a friend of yours?"

"He's nothing to me. I found him on the highway."

She touched my arm, as if to establish contact with reality, and quickly withdrew her hand, as if the contact frightened her. Her eyes were focused on my chest. I looked down at the drying smear where the bloody face had rested.

"Are you hurt, too? Can I do anything for you?"

"Not a thing," I said, and went outside.

Kerrigan was leaning in at the open back door of my car. He straightened sharply when he heard my feet in the gravel.

"Is he still breathing?"

"Yeah, he's breathing." The alcoholic blood had drained out of his face, leaving it blotched. "I don't think we ought to move him, but we'll take him inside if you say so."

"He might dirty your carpet."

"There's no need to get unpleasant, fellow. You heard me offer to take him in."

"Forget it."

He moved up closer to me, his eyes opaque and stony gray in the floodlights. "Where did you find him?"

"A couple of miles south of the Marine Base, in the ditch."

"How did you happen to bring him here, to my doorstep? If I may ask."

"You may ask. This was the first place I came to. Next time I'll keep going."

"I don't mean that. I merely wondered if it was a coincidence."

"Why? Do you know him?"

"Yeah. He drives a truck for the Meyer line in town. Name's Tony Aquista."

"You know him well?"

"I wouldn't say that. In my line of business I have a speaking acquaintance with most of the jerks in Las Cruces. But I don't hobnob with Mexican truck-drivers."

"Good for you. Any idea who shot him?"

"That's kind of a silly question."

"You could still answer it."

"What gives you the right to ask questions, fellow?"

"Go on calling me fellow. It sends me."

"You didn't mention your name."

"That's right. I didn't."

"Maybe I ought to ask you a question or two," he said. "You didn't happen to shoot him yourself by any chance?"

"You're very acute. Naturally I shot him. This is my getaway."

"I was merely asking. I couldn't help noticing the blood on you."

He smiled with soft malice. His changeable mouth, both sensitive and brutal, tempted my fist the way a magnet tempts iron. He was big enough, and not too old, but he was a little ripe. I put my fist in my pocket and walked around to the other side of the car.

I switched on the dome light. Tony Aquista was still blowing his sad small bubbles. His eyes were completely closed now. He was blind and deaf with the effort to hold onto life. The ambulance sighed in the road.

I followed it on its return trip through the highway suburbs, past motels and cabins and trailer parks where soldiers and salesmen and tourists and migrant workers passed temporary nights with temporary bedmates. At a six-lane wye where two main roads converged, the ambulance turned off the highway to the left.

I missed the green arrow and had to wait. The hospital was visible in the distance, a long white box of a building pierced with lights. Nearer the highway, the lighted screen of an outdoor theater, on which two men were beating each other to the rhythm of passionate music, rose against the night like a giant dream of violence.

I found the ambulance entrance at the rear of the hospital. Its red electric sign spelled out EMERGENCY and cast a hellish glow on the oil-stained concrete driveway. Before I went in, I took a clean shirt out of my bag and put it on.

In the receiving-room half a dozen white-coated people were grouped around the table where Tony Aquista lay. Now even his lips were yellow. An inverted bottle of blood was dripping into a tube that was strapped to his arm.

A young doctor, resident or intern, leaned over the closed face and pressed his thumbs down into the eyes. Aquista didn't stir. The room seemed to be holding its breath. I moved to the doctor's side. He glanced at me sharply.

"Are you a patient?"

"A witness. I found this man."

He shook his head from side to side. "You should have found him sooner." He turned to one of the nurses: "Don't waste any more blood on him."

She closed off the rubber tube and disconnected the half-empty bottle. The hospital smell, the odor of dissolution, was keen in my nostrils.

"Is he going, doctor?"

"He's gone. No pulse, no respiration. He must have been bleeding for some time, probably didn't have a pint left in his system."

"Bullet wound?"

"Unquestionably, I'd say. These lung wounds are murder."

I looked down at Tony Aquista's face. It had changed from flesh to wax, and the teeth were grinning.

"Murder is the word."

I must have said it loudly or strangely. The doctor gave me a compunctious look.

"This man a buddy of yours?"

"No. I just don't like to see it happen to anybody. Have you called the police?"

"The sheriff's office. It happened in the county, didn't it?"

"That's where they ditched him, anyway."

He moved to the door, saying over his shoulder: "The sheriff will want you to stick around, I expect."

I didn't tell him that waiting in sterile rooms for policemen was my calling. I waited for this one on a metal campchair outside the receiving-room. The business of the hospital went on around me. Nurses came and went, clearing the room for the next emergency case. Tony Aquista, featureless under a sheet, was trundled away to the morgue at the end of the corridor.

Part of my mind went with him into the cold darkness. It's like that sometimes when a younger man dies. I felt as if a part of me had turned to wax under the white lights.

From somewhere in the murmurous bowels of the building an infant's cry rose sharp. I wondered if it was a newborn baby equalizing the population of Las Cruces.

CHAPTER **2**:   *A tall man in a gray business suit* opened the door of the morgue. His dazzling off-white Stetson just missed the top of the doorframe as he came out. He smacked the concrete wall with the flat of his hand and said to the uniformed deputy behind him:

"God damn it, what happened to Tony?"

The deputy shrugged. "Woman trouble, maybe. You know Tony, chief."

"Yes. I know Tony."

The sheriff's striding shadow lengthened toward me. The face under the hatbrim was long and lean like his body, and burned by the valley sun. Though he was young for his job, about my age, I could see the scars of old pain branching out from the corners of his eyes and bracketing his mouth. His eyes were deepset and dark like the windows of a haunted house.

"You're the one who brought him in?"

"I'm the one."

"You're not a Las Cruces man, are you?"

"Los Angeles."

"I see." He nodded as if I had made a damaging admission. "Let's have your name and home address."

I gave him my name, Lew Archer, and my business address on Sunset Boulevard. The deputy wrote them down. The sheriff dragged a second chair up to mine and sat facing me.

"I'm Sheriff Church. This is Danelaw, my identification officer. And what's your occupation, Mr. Archer, besides acting as a good Samaritan?" If Church was trying to be genial, he wasn't succeeding.

"I'm a licensed private detective."

"Well. This is quite a coincidence. Or is it? What were you doing out on the highway?"

"Driving..I'm on my way to Sacramento."

"Not tonight," he said brusquely. "It doesn't pay to be a good Samaritan nowadays. I'm afraid you're going to have to put up with a certain amount of red tape. We'll need you for the inquest, for one thing."

"I realize that."

"I'll hurry it if I can—tomorrow or the next day. Let's see, this is Thursday. Can you stay over till Saturday?"

"If I have to."

"Good. Now how did you happen to pick him up?"

"He was lying in the ditch a couple of miles south of the Marine Base. He managed to get up onto his knees and wave at me."

"He was still conscious then? Did he say anything?"

"He lost consciousness before I got to him. I didn't like to move him, but there was no way to telephone, no one to send for help. I put him in the back seat of my car and phoned for an ambulance from the first place I came to."

"Where was that?"

"Kerrigan's motor court. Kerrigan had quite a reaction to the thing. It seems he knew Aquista, and didn't want any part of him, dead or alive. His wife called the ambulance for me."

"What was Mrs. Kerrigan doing there?"

"Holding down the desk, apparently."

"Wasn't Kerrigan's manager around? Miss Meyer?"

"If she was, I didn't see her. Does it matter?"

"No." The sheriff's voice had risen. He brought it under control. "It's the first time I ever heard of Kate Kerrigan going to work in the place."

Danelaw looked up from his notebook. "She's been out there all week."

Church looked at him as if he had more questions, but he swallowed them. His knobbed throat moved visibly.

I said: "Kerrigan was a little under the weather. Which may account for his manners. He asked me if I shot the man myself."

A tight smile pincered the sheriff's mouth. "What did you say to that?"

"No. I never saw the man before. I thought I'd get that on the record, in case he babbles some more."

"Not a bad idea, under the circumstances. Now if you'll show me the way to the spot where you found him."

We stood up at the same time. His bony hand closed on

my shoulder and urged me toward the exit. I couldn't tell whether it was a gesture of encouragement or command. In any case, I jerked my shoulder free.

His car was a new black Mercury special with undercover plates and no official markings. It followed me south out of town, the way I had come. The twilight lull in the traffic was over. It was full night now. Headlights after headlights stabbed up through the valley from the south, flashed in my eyes and away. From the north we were overtaken by a second official car.

We passed through the deserted camp and I began to watch the roadside. Spotlight beams from the cars behind me dragged in the ditch like broken oars of light. After two false stops I found the place. It was marked by a dribble of drying blood on the gravel shoulder. The bent jimson weeds below the shoulder still held the impression of a spreadeagled body.

Several deputies climbed out of the second patrol car. One of them was a bull-shouldered man with bright quick Spanish eyes moving constantly in an Indian-colored face. He gave the sheriff an impatient salute:

"Communications got in touch with Meyer. Tony was driving today all right, and the truck is missing."

"What was on the truck?"

"Meyer wouldn't say. He wants to talk to you about it. When I get my hands on the mother-lovers that did it—" The dark man's roving gaze rested on me, so hard I could feel its impact.

The sheriff laid a fatherly arm around the olive-drab shoulders. "Take it slow now, Sal. I know how you people feel about blood-relations. Tony was your cousin, wasn't he?"

"My mother's sister's son."

"We'll get the ones that did it, Sal, but we'll make sure that they're the right ones first. This man here had nothing to do with the killing. He found Tony and brought him to the hospital."

"Is that what he says?"

"That's what I say." The sheriff's tone became abruptly official. "Where's Meyer now?"

"At the yard."

"Go over to the west side and get the dope on the truck. Tell the old man I'll be along later. Put out a general alarm on it. And I want roadblocks on every road leading out of the county. Got that, Sal?"

"Yessir."

The dark-faced deputy ran to his car. The sheriff and the rest of his men went over the ground with eyes and fingers and flashbulbs.

Danelaw, the identification officer, took an impression of my shoe and checked it against the footprints in the ditch. There were no footprints except mine, and no new tire-tracks on the gravel shoulder.

"It looks as if he was dumped from a car," Church said. "Or maybe from his truck. Whatever it was, it didn't leave the concrete." He looked at me. "Did you see a car? Or a truck?"

"No."

"Nothing at all?"

"No."

"It's possible they didn't stop, just flung him out and let him lie, and he crawled off the road himself."

Danelaw spoke up from the side of the road: "I'd say that's what he did, chief. There's traces of blood where he dragged himself into the ditch."

Church spat on the concrete. "A God-damn nasty business." He turned to me, almost casually. "Can I have a look at your license, by the way?"

"Why not?" I showed him my photostat.

"It looks all right to me. And what did you say you were

going to do when you got to Sacramento?"

"I didn't say. I have a report to make to a legislative committee." I named the committee chairman. "He hired me to study narcotics distribution in the southern counties."

"If I wanted to go to the trouble of checking that story, would it check out?"

"Naturally. I have some correspondence with me."

I started for my car, but Church stopped me:

"Don't bother. You're not under suspicion. Sal Braga's an emotional bastard, and he happens to be related to Aquista. In this town everybody's related to everybody else. Which sometimes makes things a little complicated." He was silent for a moment. "What do you say we go and talk to Kerrigan?"

"It sounds delightful."

By this time the roadside was lined with cars, official and unofficial. A highway patrolman was directing traffic with a flashlight. He made room for the sheriff's Mercury to turn, and I followed in my car.

The red glow over the city reminded me of the reflection of the emergency sign at the hospital, infinitely magnified. Beyond the glowing city, in the hills, the rotating beam of an air beacon seemed to be probing the night for some kind of meaning.

CHAPTER 3: *Kerrigan must have been watching* for the sheriff. He came out of the lobby as I pulled up behind the Mercury.

"How's the boy, Brand?"

"Good enough."

They shook hands. But I noticed as they talked that each man watched the other like chess opponents who had played before. Or opponents in a deadlier game than chess. No,

Kerrigan said, he didn't know what had happened to Aquista, or why. He had seen no evil, heard no evil, done no evil. The man in the car had asked to use his telephone, and that was his sole connection with the case. He gave me a look of bland hostility.

"How's business, by the way?" Church glanced up at the no-vacancy sign, which was lit. "I guess I don't have to ask."

"As a matter of fact it's lousy. I turned that on because my wife's too upset to handle the desk. She says."

"Is Anne on her vacation?"

"You could call it that."

"Did she quit?"

Kerrigan lifted and dropped his heavy shoulders. "I wouldn't know. I was going to ask you."

"Why me?"

"She's your relative, after all. She hasn't been on the job all week, and I haven't been able to get in touch with her."

"Isn't she in her apartment?"

"The phone doesn't answer." Kerrigan peered up sharply into the sheriff's face. "Haven't you seen her either, Brand?"

"Not this week." He added after a pause: "We don't see too much of Anne any more."

"That's funny. I thought she was practically part of the family."

"You thought wrong. She and Hilda get together now and then, but mostly Anne leads her own life."

Kerrigan smiled his soft and ugly smile. "Maybe this week she's leading her own life a little more than usual, eh?"

"What does that mean?"

"Whatever you want to put into it."

Church took a long step toward him, his hands clubbed. His eyes were wide and black, and his face had a green patina in the colored light. He looked sick with anger.

I opened the car door and got one foot on the gravel.

The sound of my movement checked him. He stood shivering, staring down into Kerrigan's evil grin. Then he turned on his heel and walked away from us. He walked like a mechanical man to the margin of the light and stood there with his back to us and his head down.

"Shut my big mouth, eh?" Kerrigan said cheerfully. "He'll blow his top once too often, and blow himself out of the courthouse."

Mrs. Kerrigan opened the door of the lobby. "Is something the matter, Don?" She came toward us, wearing a silver-fox cape and an anxious expression.

"Something always is. I told the sheriff Anne Meyer didn't turn up this week. He seems to think I'm to blame. I'm not responsible for his God-damn sister-in-law."

She laid a timid hand on his arm, like somebody trying to soothe an excited animal. "You must have misunderstood him, darling. I'm sure he couldn't blame you for anything she does. He probably wants to ask her about Tony Aquista."

"Why?" I said. "Did she know Aquista, too?"

"Of course she did. He had a crush on her. Didn't he, Don?"

"Shut up."

She backed away from him, stumbling on her high heels as if she had been pushed.

"Go on, Mrs. Kerrigan. It may be important. Aquista died just now."

"He died?" Her hands went to her breast and wound themselves in the fur cape. She looked from me to her husband, her blue eyes darkening. "Is Anne mixed up in it?"

"I wouldn't know," he said. "This is enough of this, Kate. Go inside. You're cold and upset and making a fool of yourself."

"I am not. You can't order me in. I have a perfect right to talk to anyone I choose."

"You're not going to shoot off your mouth to this bastard."

"I haven't been—"

"Shut up." His voice was quiet and deadly. "You've made enough trouble for me already."

He seized her elbows from behind and half carried her to the door of the lobby. She struggled weakly in his grasp, but when he released her she went in without a backward glance.

He came back toward me, running his fingers lovingly through his hair. It was clipped in a crew cut, much too short for his age. I guessed that he was one of those middle-aging men who couldn't face the fact that their youth was over. It gave him an unreal surface, under which a current of cruelty flickered.

"You don't believe in killing them with kindness."

"I know how to handle bitches. Purebred bitches or any other kind of bitches. I also know how to handle nosy sons of bitches. Unless you're here in some official capacity, I suggest you get off my property. But quick."

I looked around for Church. He was in a public telephone booth at the end of the row of cottages. The receiver was at his ear, but he didn't seem to be talking.

"Take it up with the sheriff," I said. "I'm with him."

"Just who are you, fellow? If I thought you sicked the sheriff onto me—"

"What would happen, sweetheart?" He was my favorite man now. I kept my hands down and my chin out, hoping that he would swing and give me a chance to counter.

"You'd be flat on your back with a throatful of teeth."

"I thought you only pushed women around."

"You want a demonstration?"

But he was bluffing. From the sharp bright corners of his eyes he was watching the sheriff approach. The sheriff's face was solemn and composed:

"I owe you an apology, Don. I don't often lose my head like that."

"Don't you? You'll try it on one too many taxpayers. Then you won't be able to get yourself elected dogcatcher."

"All right. Let's bury it. I didn't hurt you."

"I'd like to see you try."

"I said bury it," Church repeated quietly. His facial muscles were anatomized by the effort he was exerting to hold himself under control. "Tell me more about Anne. Nobody seems to know where she is. She didn't tell Hilda she was quitting her job or going anywhere."

"She didn't quit the job. She just went away for the weekend and didn't show up for work Monday morning. Apparently she didn't come back from the weekend. I haven't had any word from her."

"Where did she go?"

"You tell me. She doesn't report to me."

They faced each other for a long still moment. There was something worse than potential violence between them, a hatred that went beyond violence and absorbed them completely, like a grand passion.

"You're a liar," Church said finally.

"Maybe I am a liar. Maybe it's just as well I am. If I am."

Church saw me watching them and jerked his head in peremptory command. I left them bound in their quiet vicious quarrel and went into the dark lobby.

Its darkness was barely penetrated by the green and yellow light that filtered in through the venetian blinds. Mrs. Kerrigan was curled on a lounge in the farthest corner. All I could see of her was silver-pointed hair and the wet gleam of eyes.

"Who is it?"

"Archer. The one who brought you the trouble."

"You didn't bring the trouble. I've had it all along."

She rose and came into the center of the room. "You're not on the local police force, Mr. Archer."

"No, I'm a private detective. The southern counties are my normal beat. I stumbled into this one."

"Didn't we all." Her odor was faint and fragrant, like nostalgia for half-forgotten summers. Her troubled whisper might have been the voice of the breathing darkness: "What does it all mean?"

"Your guess is better than mine. You know the people involved."

"Do I? Not really. I don't really know my own husband, even."

"How long have you been married?"

"Seven years. Seven lean years." She hesitated. "Mr. Archer, are you the sort of detective people hire, to find out things about other people?"

I told her that I was.

"Could I—can I trust you?"

"It's up to you. Other people have been able to, but I don't carry references."

"Would it cost a great deal? I have *some* money left."

"I don't know what you have in mind."

"Of course you don't. I'm sorry. I'm awfully scatter-brained tonight."

"Or else you don't want to tell me."

"That may be it." I could sense her invisible smile. "Or it may be that I don't know exactly what I want done. I certainly don't want to make trouble for anyone."

"Such as your husband?"

"Yes. My husband." Her voice dropped, almost out of hearing. "I found Don packing last night, both of his big suitcases. I believe he intends to leave me."

"Why not ask him?"

"I wouldn't dare," she said with a desolate kind of wit. "He might give me an answer."

"You're in love with him?"

"I haven't the slightest idea," she said a little wildly. "I was at one time, quite a long time ago."

"Another woman?"

"Other women, yes."

"Would Anne Meyer be one of them?"

"I know she used to be. There was a—a thing between them last year. He told me it was off, but it may still be on. If you could find her, find out whom she's seeing—" Her voice trailed off.

"Exactly how long has she been missing?"

"Since she took off for the weekend, last Friday."

"Where did she spend the weekend?"

"I don't really know."

"With your husband?"

"No. At least he says not. I was going to say—"

Kerrigan spoke behind me: "What were you going to say?"

He had quietly opened the door of the lobby. His bulky shadow moved forward out of its panel of light. He pushed past me and leaned tensely toward his wife:

"I told you not to shoot off your mouth."

"I didn't—"

"But I heard you. You wouldn't call me a liar now, would you, Kate?"

His back swung sideways. I heard the crack of the blow, and the woman's hissing gasp. I took him by the shoulder.

"Lay off her, bully boy."

The heavy wad of padding came loose in my hand, and something ripped. He let out a canine yelp and turned on me. One of his flailing fists numbed the side of my neck.

I backed into the light from the doorway and let him come to me. He charged like a ram, directly into my left. It straightened him up, and I followed through with a short right cross to the jaw. His knees buckled. He swayed forward. I hit him again with my left before his face struck the carpet.

His wife kneeled beside him. "You men. You're like horrible little boys." She cradled his head in her hands, and wiped his cut chin with a lace-edged handkerchief. "Is he badly hurt, do you think?"

"I doubt it. I didn't hit him often."

"You shouldn't have hit him at all."

"He asked for it."

"Yes. I suppose he did." Kerrigan stirred and moaned. She looked up at me fearfully. "You'd better get out of here now. Don has a gun and he knows how to use it."

"Did he use it on Aquista?"

"Certainly not. That's ridiculous." Her voice was high and defensive. "My husband had nothing to do with it. He was here with me all afternoon."

Kerrigan struggled groggily in her arms, trying to sit up. "Please go now," she said without looking at me.

"What about the job we were discussing?"

"We'll simply have to forget it. I can't stand any more trouble."

"Whatever you say. It's your marriage."

CHAPTER 4: *The sheriff's Mercury was gone, and* the floodlit gravel was like a deserted arena. I wheeled my own car out onto the highway and joined the citybound traffic, not for long. An indefinable feeling of relationship pulled at me like a long elastic tying me to the Kerrigans and their trouble. Call it curiosity; but Mrs. Kerrigan's oblique blond beauty had a lot to do with it. I wanted to see her out of trouble, and her husband in deeper trouble.

The elastic reached the limit of its stretch and pulled my car to a stop on the shoulder. A break in the traffic let me make a U-turn. I drove back past the motor court, U-turned again a hundred yards beyond it, and parked in the deep shade of a roadside oak.

I smoked two cigarettes. Then the floodlights around the motor court were extinguished. The green and yellow sign was plunged into darkness. I turned on my ignition and pressed the starter.

The lobby windows went dark, and Kerrigan emerged. Taking noticeably short steps, he crossed the gravel to an alley that ran behind the row of cottages. A minute later his fire-engine-red convertible appeared at the mouth of the alley. He honked impatiently. Mrs. Kerrigan came out, holding her silver fox around her shoulders, and ran to the convertible.

It was an easy car to tail. I followed it into Las Cruces and across the city to a hillside residential section. There Kerrigan dropped his wife in front of a big two-story house set on a terraced slope. I noted its location.

Kerrigan turned back toward the center of town, driving as if his car was an engine of destruction. He parked it eventually on a side street near Main. I found a space for my own car and went after him on foot.

We were in the lower reaches of the downtown section, an urban wasteland of cheap hotels, rummage and second-hand-furniture shops, Mexican and Chinese restaurants. Kerrigan paused under a café sign: SAMMY's ORIENTAL GARDENS, and started to look up and down the street. I stepped into the doorway of a hockshop. Its feebly lit interior lay behind barred windows like an insane memory of civilization.

When I stepped out onto the sidewalk, Kerrigan was gone. I double-timed to the front of the café and looked in through the fly-specked plate glass. He was walking toward the rear of the place, escorted by a Chinese waiter who beckoned him smilingly through a curtained archway. I waited until he was out of sight, and went in.

It was a big old-fashioned restaurant with a crowded bar along one side and wooden booths on the other, painted black and orange. Unlit paper lanterns hung dismally from the smoky pressed-iron ceiling. A languid ceiling fan stirred an atmosphere compounded of rancid grease and soy sauce, whisky-laden breath and human sweat. The people were from the lower echelons of valley life: oilfield roughnecks and their women, cowpokes in high-heeled riding boots, an old rumdum sitting in a booth in alcoholic isolation, waiting for dreams to begin.

The Chinese waiter came forward from the rear and showed me his teeth and gums.

"You wish a booth, sir?" he said precisely.

"I'd prefer a private room."

"Sorry, sir, it's been taken. If you had come one minute earlier."

"It doesn't matter."

I sat down in one of the front booths so that I could watch the archway in the mirror behind the bar. The waiter called for a double rye on the rocks and carried it out through the archway. When he brought me my menu I said:

"Those paper lanterns are a fire hazard, aren't they? I'm a little nervous about fires. Does this building have a rear exit?"

"No, sir, but it's perfectly safe. We've never had a fire. Do you wish to order now, sir?"

I remembered that I hadn't eaten since noon, and ordered a bottle of beer and a New York cut. Fit for a King, the menu said, So Bring Your Queen. It lied.

I was washing down the last leathery shreds of the steak with beer when a girl sauntered in from the street. Her head was small and beautifully molded, capped with short black hair like glistening satin. She had flat black eyes, a mouth as sullen as sin. Her mink-dyed rabbit coat hung open, and her hips swayed as she walked to an obvious rhythm.

Every man at the bar, including the Filipino bartender, was simultaneously aware of her. She loitered near the entrance, soaking up their awareness as if it was a fuel or a food. Her soft tiny-waisted body seemed to swell and luxuriate, and her breasts rose against the pressure of eyes.

My eyes met hers. I couldn't help smiling at her. She gave me a scornful look, and turned to the waiter:

"Is he here?"

"He just came in, miss. He's waiting for you in the back room."

I watched her sway out after him, wondering if she could be Anne Meyer. She didn't look like any motel manager I had ever seen. More likely an actress who hadn't quite made the grade down south, or a very successful amateur tart on the verge of turning pro. Whatever her business was, there had to be sex in it. She was as full of sex as a grape is full of juice, and so young that it hadn't begun to sour.

I waited until the waiter had disappeared through the swinging door to the kitchen. Then I got up and moved to the curtained archway. The corridor beyond it was narrow and ill-lit, with doors marked MEN and LADIES at the far end. A nearer doorway was hung with a thick green curtain, through which I could hear a muffled conversation. I leaned on the wall beside it.

The girl's voice said: "Was that your wife on the phone? I never talked to her before. She's got a very educated diction."

"She's educated, all right. Too damn educated." Kerrigan let out a mirthless snort. "You shouldn't have telephoned me at the court. She caught me packing my bags last night, I'm afraid she's catching on."

"To us, you mean?"

"To everything."

"Does it matter? There's nothing she can do to stop us."

"You don't know her," he said. "She's still stuck on me, in a way. And every little thing matters right now. I shouldn't be here."

"Aren't you glad to see me?"

"Of course I'm glad to see you. I just think we should have waited."

"I waited all day, Donny. I didn't hear from you, I didn't have any weed, and my nerves were screaming. I had to see you. I had to know what happened."

"Nothing happened. It worked. It's all over."

"Then we can go? Now?" She sounded young and eager.

"Not yet. I have things to do. I have to contact Bozey—"

"Isn't he gone?"

"He better not be. He still owes me money."

"He'll pay you. You can trust him, Bozey's no con man. When do you see him?"

"Later. He isn't the only one I've got to see."

"When you see him, will you do something for me, Donny?" Her voice was a kittenish mew. "Ask him for a couple of reefers for me? I can get plenty in Mexico, only I need them now, tonight. I can't stand this waiting."

"You think I'm enjoying the strain?" Self-pity whined in his tone. "It's tearing me apart. I can hardly sit still. If I wasn't crazy I wouldn't be here at all."

"Don't worry, honey. Nothing can happen here. Sammy knows about us."

"Yeah. How many other people know about us? And how much do they know? There was a private detective snooping around the motor court—"

"Forget about it, Donny." The kitten in her throat was purring now. "Come over here and tell me about the place. You know? How we'll lie in the sun all day without any clothes and have fun and watch the birds and the clouds and have servants to wait on us. Tell me about that."

I heard his feet on the floor and looked in through the narrow crack between the doorframe and the edge of the curtain. He was standing behind her chair with a doped expression on his face, a Band-aid cross on his chin. His hands moved downward from her neck.

She put her hands over his and lifted one of them to her mouth. It came away red-smeared. Kerrigan bent over her face, his fingers plucking at her clothes like a dying man at his sheets.

A sibilant voice said behind me: "Looking for something, sir?"

The Chinese waiter was in the archway, balancing a tray on which a pair of steaks sizzled.

"The men's room?"

"At the end of the hall, sir." His smile looked ready to bite me. "It's plainly marked."

"Thank you. I'm very shortsighted."

"Don't mention it, sir."

I went to the men's room and used it. When I came out, the private room was empty. The steaks sat untouched on the table with Kerrigan's empty glass. I went out through the restaurant. The Chinese waiter was behind the bar.

"Where did they go?" I said.

He looked at me as if he had never seen me before, and answered in singsong Chinese.

Outside, the street was deserted. Kerrigan's red convertible had left its parking place. I circled the block in my car, fruitlessly, and widened the circle to take in several blocks. Near the corner of Main and a street called Yanonali, I saw the girl walking in a westerly direction on Yanonali.

She was by herself, but her body swayed and swung as if she had an audience. I double-parked to let her get well ahead, then crawled along in second half a block behind her. The pavement and the buildings deteriorated as we left the downtown section. Dilapidated flats and boarding-houses whose windows gave fleeting glimpses of permanent depression were interspersed with dim little bars and sand-wich counters. The people in the bars and on the streets, brown and black and dirty gray, had dim and dilapidated personalities to match the buildings. All but the girl I was following. She swaggered along through the lower depths of the city as if she was drunk with her own desirability.

Street lights were few and far between. On a corner un-der one of them a gang of Negro boys too young for the bars were horsing in the road, projecting their black identi-ties against the black indifference of the night. They froze when the girl went by, looking at her from eyes like wet brown stones. She paid no attention to them.

In the middle of the next block she entered the lobby of an apartment building. I parked near the corner and sur-veyed the building from the other side of the street. It was big for the street, three-storied, and had once been fairly pretentious. Tile facing surmounted its stucco cornice. Its second- and third-floor windows were masked with shallow wrought-iron balconies.

But the dark tides of Yanonali Street had lapped at its foundations and surrounded it with an atmosphere of hope-lessness. A patched earthquake scar zigzagged across its face. Yellow rust-streaks ran down from the balconies like iron tears. The lights behind the blinded windows, the ill-lit lobby open on the street, gave an impression of furtive transiency.

I didn't know the girl's name, and she would be almost impossible to find in the warren of the building's rooms and corridors. I went back to my car. The Negro boys were standing around it on the road in a broken semi-circle.

"How fast will she go?" the smallest one said.

"I've hit the peg a couple of times. A hundred. Who was the girl that just went past, the one in the fur coat?"

They looked at each other blankly.

"We don't pay no mind to girls," the tallest one said.

"You want a girl? Trotter can get you a girl," the smallest one said. "He got six sisters." He performed a brief skinny-hipped hula.

The tall one kicked him sharply in the rear. "You silence yourself, my sisters is all working."

The small one skipped out of his reach. "Sure. They working night and day." He did a couple of bumps.

I said: "Where's the Meyer truck line?"

"I thought he wanted a girl," one of them said to the other. "Now he wants a truck. He can't make up his mind."

"Keep right on going west," the tall one said. "You know where the big overpass is?"

"No."

"Well, you'll see it, off to the left. Meyer's is on the other side of the highway."

I thanked him and gave him a dollar. The others watched the transaction with the same bright stony look that they had given the girl. As I drove away, a tin can rattled on my turtleback. Their rattling laughter followed me down the street.

CHAPTER 5: *The road bumped over railroad* tracks, twisted through pine-smelling lumberyards, ducked under the overpass that carried the highway. Night-running trucks went over my head like thunder. The Meyer yard was almost in the shadow of the overpass, a black-top square hemmed in by high wire fence ⸱ nd flanked by a storage building. A truck was backed in to the loading dock, another stood under an open-sided shelter supported on concrete columns, and two others were parked inside the gate. The gate was open. I drove through and pulled up at the platform.

A bald man in an oil-stained T-shirt was sitting on a packing case at the back of the platform. A thousand-watt bulb over the door of the warehouse held him in pitiless light. He was freckled and blotched all over, head and neck and arms, as if his maker had flicked a paintbrush at him. His scarred brown hands were rolling a Bull Durham cigarette. When I got out of the car, his pinkish lashless eyes moved in my direction.

"What can I do for you, bud?"

"I'd like to see Mr. Meyer."

"Meyer ain't here. He went off with his son-in-law."

"His son-in-law?"

"Brand Church. The sheriff. Maybe you can catch him at home. Is it business?"

"More or less. I hear you lost a rig."

"That's right." He licked the edge of his tan cigarette paper and pressed it into place. "And a driver."

"What kind of a rig?"

"Twenty-ton semi-trailer." He lit a kitchen match with his thumbnail and held it to his cigarette. "Cost the old man forty grand last year."

"What was it carrying?"

He came to the edge of the platform, blinking down at me suspiciously. "I wouldn't know. The old man told me not to talk about it."

"Why not?"

"He's sore as a boil. The rig and the payload was both insured, but when a firm loses a truck, shippers start getting

leery." He glanced at the license number on the front
of my car. "You from a newspaper?"

"Not me."

"The bonding company?"

"Guess again." I climbed up the concrete steps to the
platform. "What was the payload?"

Turning quickly, he stepped inside the open back of the
truck and came out with a long curved piece of steel like
a blunt saber. He swung the tire-iron idly in his hand. "I
don't know you. Now what's your interest?"

"Take it easy—"

"The hell. A chum of mine gets shot like a dog in the
road and you tell me to take it easy. What's your interest?"

His voice was a fox-terrier yap, a high bark that sounded
strange coming from a body like a flayed bear's. The tire-
iron swung faster, moving in a tight circle beside his leg.
The muscles in his arm knotted and swelled like angry
speckled snakes.

I lifted my weight forward onto the balls of my feet,
ready to move either way. "Take it hard, then. I found your
friend on the highway. I didn't like it, either."

"You found Tony after they killed him?"

"He wasn't dead when I picked him up. He died at the
hospital a few minutes later."

"Did he say anything, tell you who drilled him?"

"Tony wasn't talking. He was unconscious, in deep shock.
My interest is finding the people that did it to him."

"You a cop? State police?" His iron weapon was still,
forgotten in his hand.

"I've worked for the state police. I'm a private detective."

"Old man Meyer hire you?"

"Not yet."

"You think he's going to?"

"If he's smart."

"That's what you think. Meyer still has his first nickel."
His rubbery mouth stretched in a broken-toothed grin. He
laid the iron on the packing case behind him, ready to his
hand.

I reached for my cigarettes, then thought better of it.
"I'm out of smokes. Can I roll one?"

"Sure thing."

He handed me his tobacco and papers and watched me
critically while I rolled a cigarette. My fingers remembered
the knack. He lit it for me.

"So you're a detective, eh?"

"That's right. My name is Archer."

"Tarko." He thumbed his chest. "They call me Hairless."

"Glad to meet you, Tarko. What was Tony's run?"

"It varied. Mostly he drove the San Francisco run. He
was coming up from L.A. today, though. Special shipment."

"What kind of a truck was he driving?"

"One of the new semis, GMC tractor, Fruehauf box. A
twenty-tonner, same as that one there."

He pointed across the yard with his cigarette, to one of
the trucks that were standing inside the gate. It was a closed
semi-trailer the size of a small house. Its corrugated metal
sides were bright with aluminum paint, except for the red
and black sign: MEYER LINE—LOCAL AND LONG DISTANCE—
LAS CRUCES, CALIF.

"And the payload?" I said.

"You'll have to ask the old man. I'm not supposed to
know. I'm just watchman here since I had my accidents."

"But you do know?"

He didn't answer for a minute. He looked behind him,
then up at the long lighted arc of the overpass where the
big night trucks were rolling, southward to Los Angeles and
the Imperial Valley, northward to Fresno, San Francisco,
Portland. His eyes glazed with desire. He wished that he

was rolling, headed north for Portland or south or east, anywhere so long as he was wheeling with horsepower under his toe.

"Can you keep it under your hat?"

I told him I could.

He lowered his voice. "I heard the old man talking to the sheriff. He said it was bonded bourbon."

"The whole truckload?"

"Must have been. The load alone was insured for sixty-five gees."

"Was Tony bonded?"

"For a hundred, yep. He's our bonded driver. I thought at first you was from the bonding company. The first idea they ever get in their little pointed heads is jumping on our necks."

"Tony's in the clear, anyway."

"Yeah. But I can't figure it. He had his orders not to stop for anybody or anything. The old man always says we shouldn't stop for the Governor himself if he wanted a lift. Anybody tries to cut over on us, we're supposed to bull on through, smash them if we have to." He brought his right fist up and smacked the inside of his other hand. "Only way I can see it, Tony forgot his orders and stopped on the highway for somebody. The poor little son of gun." His left hand clenched his fist in a grip that left fingernail marks.

"You were fond of Tony."

"Call it that. We live—we lived in the same boarding-house. I liked him better than most. I owed him something. The time my brakes went out on the Nojoqui grade, he was my helper. I was driving a tanker full of high-octane stuff. Took the ditch at a hundred. Tony jumped out at the top of the hill and ran the hell down and pulled me out of it. All I lost was my hair."

"Who would he stop for?" I said. "I heard he liked women."

"Who doesn't?" He smiled ruefully. "The broads run like a deer when I take off my hat now."

I brought him back to the subject: "What about Tony's women? Drivers have been fingered by a woman before."

"You're telling me." He was quiet for a moment, thinking hard. "There was a dame, yeah. I don't hardly like to say it. I don't know nothing against the dame for sure."

"It wouldn't be a woman called Anne Meyer?"

"Annie Meyer? Hell, no. She's Meyer's daughter. What would she be doing fingering one of her old man's trucks?"

"I understood that she was Tony's love interest."

"She was in a way, I guess. He talked about her a lot. Sure, he was stuck on her. But she could never see him. Annie's got other interests. That was the big sorrow in his life. But it didn't amount to anything real. Know what I mean? This other dame was different. She made a big play for Tony the last week or so. He told me she was nuts about him. I dunno. It appeared to me he was stepping out of his class, same as he tried to do with Annie Meyer. The dame is a nightclub singer, a real doll. I never see her, but he showed me her picture in the front of the club."

"In town here?"

"Yeah. The Slipper, out at the end of Yanonali Street. He spent a lot of time there the last few days. And the way he talked, he'd stop a truck for her." It was the highest compliment he could pay.

"What was her name?"

"I don't remember her last name. Tony called her Jo." He massaged his scalp. "The thing that makes me suspicious, she fell for Tony awful hard and fast, and she must of had a reason."

"He was a good-looking boy, if she liked the Latin type."

"Yeah. Sure. I'll tell you, though, dames didn't go for Tony usually. He frightened them off, kind of—got too in-

tense about it, you might say. When he went overboard for
some beast, he couldn't leave her alone. Like with Annie
Meyer now." He paused and looked behind him. The
lighted warehouse was empty, except for piles of cases along
the walls.

"What about her?"

"Nothing much. He got in a little trouble over her. I guess
I shouldn't be flapping at the mouth. Only you brought
her up."

"Did he get too intense about her?"

"You can say that twice. But what do you say we skip
it? The guy's dead now. He won't be bothering women any
more. He never did mean them any harm. And most ways
he was a decent guy for a Mex, as straight as any white
man." He searched his mind for an illustration, and added:
"He had a damn good record on the road."

"This trouble he got into over Annie Meyer," I said.
"What kind of trouble was it?"

Tarko looked uncomfortable. "Tony was a little bit of a
nut, see. Just about dames, I mean. Especially Annie. She
let him take her out a couple of times last year, and then
he got in the habit of following her around at night, peep-
ing in her apartment window, stuff like that. The poor guy
didn't mean any harm, but he got himself picked up for it."

"Who picked him up?"

"The sheriff. He gave Tony a tongue-lashing, said he was
nuts and he ought to go and see a head-doctor. Tony told
me all about it at the time."

My handmade cigarette was out. I dropped it and ground
it under my heel. It had served its purpose.

"About this girl of his—Jo—did you give the sheriff the
dope on her?"

"Not me. I wouldn't give the chicken sheriff the time of
day."

"You don't seem to like the sheriff much."

"I know Brand Church too well. He drove a truck for the old man one summer when he was in college. I knew him way back before that, even, when his father ran a barbershop downtown. Brand was all right in those days, he was a damn good football-player in high school. Only going to college changed him. He came back to town with a lot of big ideas."

"What kind of big ideas?"

"Psychology, he called it. Everybody was crazy except him. Hell, he even tried to pull it on me, said that I was accident-prone or something. He as much as told me I ought to get my head examined. Me." An old anger reddened his scalp, blotchily. "Maybe he can put it over on the rest of the town. I don't buy it. The old man don't like him much, either, but he's stuck with him for a son-in-law."

"How many daughters has Meyer got?"

"Just the two. Church married the older one, Hilda. She was helping around the office that same summer, and she went for him. I never could figure out why. The old man raised a hell of a stink about it."

"Where does the old man live?"

He gave me directions, and nudged me confidentially with his shoulder. "Don't tell him what I said, eh? I like a guy that can roll his own, and I talk too much sometimes."

I thanked him for his information and told him I could hold it.

CHAPTER **6**:   *Meyer lived in a big frame house* that stood against a eucalyptus grove at the rear of a vacant lot. The lot wasn't entirely vacant. Eight or nine car bodies, T-models, A-models, an old Reo truck, and a pickup lay among its weeds in various stages of disintegration.

I left my car in the driveway and crossed the rank lawn, circling a concrete fishpond whose stagnant smell competed with the uric odor of the eucalyptus trees. The old-fashioned deep veranda was shadowy and cluttered with garden tools and tangled hose. Its boards creaked under my feet.

A sharper sound split the silence, twice, three times. I tried the front door. It was locked. Three more shots cracked out, from somewhere deep inside the house, probably the basement. Between them I heard the tap-tap of approaching footsteps. A woman's voice said through the door: "Is that you, Brand?"

I didn't answer. A light went on over my head and she pulled the heavy door open. "Oh. I'm sorry. I was expecting my husband."

She was a tall woman, still young, with a fine head of chestnut air. Her body leaning awkwardly in the doorway was heavy-breasted and very female, almost too female for comfort.

"Mrs. Church?"

"Yes. Have we met somewhere?"

Her malachite-green eyes searched my face, but they were only half-focused. They seemed to be looking through me or beyond me for something in the outside darkness, someone she feared or loved.

"I've met your husband," I said. "What's all the shooting about?"

"It's only father. When something upsets him, he likes to go down in the basement and shoot at a target."

"I don't have to ask you what upset him. In fact, I want to talk to him about the truck he lost." I told her my name and occupation. "May I come in?"

"If you like. I warn you, the house is a mess. I have my own house to look after, and I can't do much for Father's.

I've tried to get him to have a woman in, but he won't have a woman in the house."

She opened the door wider and stood to one side. Stepping in past her, I gave her a close look. If she had known how to groom herself, she could have been beautiful. But her thick hair was chopped off in girlish bangs, which made her face seem wide. Her dress was too young and it hung badly on her, parodying her figure.

She backed away from my gaze like a shy child, turned quickly, and went to a door at the end of the hallway. She called down a lighted stairway:

"Father, there's someone to see you."

A rough bass answered: "Who is it?"—punctuated by a single shot.

"He says that he's a detective."

"Tell him to wait."

Five more shots sounded under the floor. I felt their vibration through the soles of my shoes. The woman's body registered each one. When they had ceased she still lingered in the upslanting light from the basement stairway, as if the shots had been an overture to music I couldn't hear. A strange wild music that rang in her head and echoed along her nerves and held her rapt.

Heavy feet mounted the stairs. She backed away from the man who appeared in the light. There was something strange in her eyes, hatred or fear or the last of the silent music. He looked at her with a kind of puzzled contempt.

"Yeah, I know, Hilda. You don't like the sound of gunfire. You can always stuff cotton in your ears."

"I didn't say anything, Father. This is Mr. Archer."

He faced me under a deerhead, a big old wreck of a man who had started to shrink in his skin. His shoulders were bowed and his chest caving under a wrinkled horsehide jacket. White glinted in the reddish stubble on his cheeks and chin, and his eyes were rimmed with red. They smoldered in his head like the last vestiges of inextinguishable and ruinous passions.

"What can I do for you, Mr. Archer?" His grooved, stubborn mouth denied his willingness to do anything for anybody.

I told him I had stumbled into the case and wanted to stay in it. I didn't tell him why. I didn't know exactly why, though Kate Kerrigan had something to do with it. And perhaps the dark boy's death had become a symbol of the senseless violence I had seen and heard about in the valley towns. Here was my chance to get to the bottom of it.

"You mean you want me to hire you?" Meyer said.

"I'm giving you the opportunity."

"Some opportunity. My daughter's husband—he's the sheriff—is out on the roads right now with thirty deputies. And don't think I'm not paying them, in taxes. What have you got to sell that they can't give me?"

"Full-time attention to the case, my brains, and my guts."

"You think you're pretty hot, eh?"

"I have a reputation down south. Not a very pleasant one, but a good one in my line."

"I wouldn't know about that." He looked down at his grained hands, flexing the big-jointed fingers. I could smell the smokeless powder on them. "I *work* for my money, boy. I don't lay none of it on the line unless I see value received first. What do I stand to gain? The truck's insured, so's the payload."

"What about your standing with the shippers? These things are hard on business."

"You're telling me." He thrust his gray head forward. "Who you been talking to? Has Kerrigan been griping?"

"Where does he come in?"

"It's Kerrigan's whisky they lifted."

"You mean he owns the payload?"

"In a way. It was billed to him from the distributors. But

unless he gets delivery, I'm the one that has to take the loss."

"You said it was insured."

"Ninety per cent insured. I didn't have full coverage. The other ten comes out of my pocket." He grimaced painfully, as if he was describing a surgical operation that he faced, a moneyectomy. "Seven thousand dollars more or less."

"I'll work for ten per cent of the ten per cent. Seven hundred if I get the load back."

"And if you don't?"

"One hundred for expenses. Paid now."

He stood in front of me, shifting his weight from one leg to the other. His voice was like a wood rasp rubbing constantly on a single theme. "That's a lot of money. How do I know you'll do anything to earn it?"

"Because I'm telling you. Take it or leave it."

He smiled for the first time, foxily. "I hear you telling me. Okay, I'll make you a deal. Come in and sit down."

His living-room was the kind of room you find in back-country ranch-houses where old men hold the last frontier against women and civilization and hygiene. The carpets and furniture were glazed with dirt. Months of wood ashes clogged the fireplace and sifted onto the floor. The double-barreled shotgun over the mantel was the only clean and cared-for object in the room.

He sat on the swaybacked davenport and motioned me to a chair. "Tell you the deal I have in mind. Seven hundred for the truck and the load. Nothing for nothing."

"Aren't you pretty business-as-usual, for a man who lost a driver and a truck? Not to mention a daughter."

"What daughter are you talking about?"

"Anne. She's missing."

"You're crazy. She works for Kerrigan."

"Not any more. She dropped out of sight last Friday,

according to Mrs. Kerrigan. They haven't seen her all week."

"Why doesn't anybody tell me these things?" He raised his voice in a querulous shout: "Hilda! Where the hell are you?"

She appeared in the doorway, wearing an apron that curved like a full sail over her breast.

"What is it, Father? I'm trying to clean out the kitchen." She came forward hesitantly, looking at him and around the room as if she had wandered into an animal's lair. "Everything in the house is filthy."

"Forget about that. Where's your sister taken herself off to? Is she in trouble again?"

"Anne in trouble?"

"That's what I'm asking you. You see more of her than I do. Everybody in town sees more of her than I do."

"It's your own fault if you don't see her, and she's not in any trouble that I know of."

"Have you talked to her lately?"

"Not this week. We had lunch together one day last week."

"When?" I said.

"Wednesday."

"Did she say anything about leaving her job?"

"No. Has she quit?"

"Apparently," Meyer said. He went to the telephone that stood on a desk in the corner of the room, and dialed a number.

Hilda looked at me anxiously. "Has something happened to Anne?"

"Let's not jump to conclusions. You wouldn't have a picture of her around, a recent picture?"

"I have at home, of course. I don't know if Father has. I'll see." She moved to the door on white flitting legs as if she was glad to escape from the room.

Meyer dropped the receiver. He turned to me with his hands open, the palms held forward in a helpless gesture. "She don't answer. Doesn't Kerrigan know where she is?"

"He says not."

"You think he's lying?"

"I got the idea from his wife."

"Don't tell me she's waking up after all these years. I thought he had her buffaloed for keeps."

"I wouldn't know," I said cautiously. "Who is this Kerrigan?"

"A phony, in my opinion. He come to town along toward the end of the last war, had a job at the Marine Base— public-relations officer or something like that. He was younger then, and a lot of the girls went for the uniform and the big line. Annie wasn't the only one."

He had said too much, and covered quickly: "Look at the girl he married, Judge Craig's daughter. She come from one of the best families in town if that means anything, but Kerrigan got her dancing to his tune. He sold off the Craig ranch property the first year they were married, and went into real estate. Then he shifted to the liquor business. Then he decided there was more money in motels. He's no businessman, I can tell you that. I gave him five years when he started. Well, he's lasted seven so far."

"How's his credit?"

"Pretty shaky, I hear."

"Seventy thousand dollars' worth of bourbon is a big order for a man with a bad credit rating."

"Biggest I ever handled for him. But that ain't my worry. They tell me what they want hauled and I haul it."

"Do you do all his hauling?"

"Far as I know."

"Did he know what driver you were going to use?"

"I guess he did at that. Tony's the only one bonded for that amount." His small eyes peered at me from under

bunched gray eyebrows. "What kind of lines are you thinking along, boy? You think he 'jacked his own whisky?"

"It's a possibility."

"If I thought that, I'd cut out his liver and lights and
eat them for breakfast."

"It's a little early to plan a menu," I said. "I need more
facts. Right now I need a hundred dollars from you."

"Damn it, I thought you forgot about that."

He turned his back on me, but I caught a glimpse of his
roll. It would have choked a brontosaurus. He thrust it
back into his jacket pocket and buttoned the leather flap.
Two reluctant fifties changed hands.

"Anything else?"

"As a matter of fact, there is. About your daughter Anne,
has she been in trouble before?"

"Nothing serious. Just the usual." He sounded a little
defensive. "Annie was a motherless girl, see. Me and Hilda
did the best we could, but we couldn't always control her.
She ran with a·fast crowd in high school, and after she went
to work she spent more than she earned. I had to bail her
out a couple of times."

"How long has she worked for Kerrigan?"

"Three-four years. She started as his secretary. Then he
gave her a course in management down south so she could
run his motel business. I wanted her to come home and
keep my books for me, only that wasn't good enough for
Annie. She wanted a life of her own, she said. Well, she's
got it."

"What kind of a life has she got?"

"Don't ask me." He hefted the twin burdens of his
shoulders. "Annie left me when she was fifteen and I hardly
seen her since. Only time I do is when she wants something."

He shuffled to the fireplace and stood looking down into
the dead ashes. The light from the naked ceiling fixture

fell on his head like the glare of loneliness.

"Annie never cared about me, neither of them ever cared about me. Sure, Hilda comes and sees me once in two-three months. Probably her husband puts her up to it, so he'll inherit the business when digger gets me. Well, he can wait, the bastard can wait." He turned and announced in a loud, hoarse voice: "I'm going to live to be a hundred, see."

"Congratulations."

"You think it's funny?"

"I'm not laughing."

"Laugh if you want to. I come from a long-lived family and I'll have the last laugh, boy. Digger won't get me for a long time yet." His feelings shifted suddenly, away from himself: "What about Annie? Is she mixed up in this some way?"

"It was your idea. There may be something in it. She's close to Kerrigan, and pretty close to Aquista, I understand."

"You understand wrong. Tony was stuck on her, all right. She couldn't see him for sour apples. Hell, she was scared of him. She came around here one night last year, she wanted—" He paused, and looked at me warily.

"Wanted what?"

"Something to protect herself with. The guy was bothering her, making a nuisance out of himself, and it was getting her down. I told her I'd fire him and run him out of town, only she couldn't see that. She's a pretty soft-hearted kid in her way. So I gave her what she asked for."

"A gun?"

"Yeah, an old .38 revolver that I had." He caught and answered my silent question: "Anne didn't shoot him with it, if that's what you're thinking. All she wanted was something to protect herself from him. It just goes to show that Tony was a big nothing to her."

"Is Kerrigan?"

"I wouldn't know about that." But his eyes clouded with embarrassment.

"Have they been living together?"

"I guess so." The words came hard, forced from the bitter mouth. "I heard last year that he was paying the rent on her apartment."

"Who are you talking about?" Hilda said from the doorway.

He looked at her sideways, swinging his head like a bull. "Kerrigan. Annie and Kerrigan."

"It's a lie." She came toward us, pale and stiff with emotion. "You should be ashamed of yourself, passing on that rotten lie. The people in this town will say anything about each other. Anything."

"I was ashamed all right. Not for myself. What could I do about it? There was no way I could stop her."

"There was nothing to stop," she said to me. "It was all a lot of gossip. Anne wouldn't have anything to do with a married man."

"That's not the way I heard it," the old man said.

"Hold your dirty tongue." She turned on him like a hissing cat. "Anne is a good girl, in spite of everything that you could do. I know you tried to corrupt her—"

He took a step toward her, the back of his neck creased and reddening. "*You* hold your tongue, hear."

An electric arc of hatred flared between them. He hunched his shoulders threateningly. Hilda raised one arm to defend her face, which was radiant with fear. She was holding a rectangle of shiny paper in her upflung hand.

Meyer snatched it from her. "Where did you get this?"

"It was stuck in your bureau mirror."

"You stay out of my room."

"With pleasure. It smells like a bear-cage."

He shrugged her off and looked down at the snapshot,

shielding it like a match-flame with his hands. I asked him to let me see it. He passed it to me unwillingly, handling it like money.

The girl in the snapshot was sitting against a white boulder on a sun-drenched beach, holding her legs as if she loved their shape. Her curly dark hair was windblown, and she was laughing. She bore some resemblance to her sister, though she was prettier. She bore no resemblance at all to the girl I had seen with Kerrigan.

"What color is her hair, Mrs. Church?"

"Brown, reddish brown, a little lighter than mine."

"And how old is she?"

"Let me see. Anne's seven years younger than I am. Twenty-five."

"Is this a recent picture?"

"Fairly recent. Brandon took it last summer at Pismo Beach." She looked at her father with cold curiosity. "I didn't know you had a print of it."

"There's a lot of things you don't know."

"I wonder."

Her ice-green eyes stared him down. He crossed the room to the desk in the corner and started to fill a pipe from a half-pound tin. Somewhere outside, a car engine purred.

Hilda lifted her head and went to the window. "That must be Brandon now." Headlights slid along the street and vanished. "No, it wasn't Brandon. Didn't you say he was going to call for me?" she asked her father.

"If he could make it. He's pretty busy tonight."

"I think I'll take a taxi. It's getting late."

"It's a two-dollar fare," he said dubiously. "I'd drive you myself, only I can't leave the telephone. Why don't you take the old Chevvy? I'm not using it."

I said: "I'll be glad to drop you off."

"Oh no, you're very kind, but I couldn't."

"Sure you could, Hilda. Mr. Archer don't mind. He was just leaving anyway."

She shrugged her shoulders helplessly. Meyer regarded me with satisfaction. At least he was getting something for his money.

"Good night, Father."

"Good night, Hildie. Thanks for coming to see me."

He stayed in his corner like a tired old bull in his *querenzia*.

CHAPTER 7 :   *I backed out past the stalled, rusting* cavalcade in the vacant lot and turned east toward the center of the city. Hilda let out a sigh that sounded as if she had been holding it in for some time.

"It's really too bad. I come to visit him with the best intentions, but we always manage to quarrel. Tonight it was Anne. There always seems to be something."

"He's fairly difficult, isn't he?"

"Yes, especially with us. Anne can't get along with him at all. I don't blame her, either. She has good reason—" She caught herself up short and changed the subject: "We live on the far side of town, Mr. Archer, in the foothills. I'm afraid it's a long drive."

"I don't mind. I wanted to talk to you anyway, in private."

"About my sister?"

"Yes. Has she gone away like this before, for a week at a time?"

"Once or twice she has. But not without telling me."

"You two are pretty close, aren't you?"

"We always have been. We're not like some sisters I know, fighting all the time. Even if she is better-looking than I am—"

"I wouldn't say that."

"You don't have to be gallant. I know. Anne's a beauty, and I'm not. But it never seemed to matter much. She's so much younger, really, I never needed to compete with her. I was more like an aunt than a sister when she was growing up. Mother died when she was born, you see. She was my responsibility."

"Was she hard to handle?"

"Of course not. Don't listen to Father. He's always been prejudiced, willing to believe anything against her. That stinking gossip he told you about Anne and Mr. Kerrigan—there's nothing in it at all."

"You're sure?"

"Perfectly sure. I'd know if it was true. It isn't true," she said vehemently. "Anne worked for Mr. Kerrigan, and that's all."

I pulled up behind a line of cars that was waiting for the light to change at the main street intersection. Single men and couples, boys in threes and fours, roved on the lighted pavements, their faces bored and hungry for excitement. No unescorted women were to be seen.

"Keep going on this street," she said. "I'll tell you where to turn."

The light winked green, and we rolled forward across the pitted asphalt.

"Where does your sister live when she's at home?"

"She has her own apartment, in Bougainvillea Court, number three. It's not far from here, on Los Bagnos Street."

"I may go over there later. I don't suppose you have a key?"

"No, I don't. Why do you want a key?"

"I'd like to have a look at her possessions. They might give some indication of where she's gone, and why."

"I see. No doubt the superintendent can let you in."

"Do I have your permission?"

"Certainly." She was silent for a while, as we passed through sparsely lighted streets toward the edge of the city. "Where do you think Anne has gone, Mr. Archer?"

"I was going to ask you. I have no idea, unless you're mistaken about her and Kerrigan."

"I couldn't be mistaken," she said bluntly. "Why keep harping on that?"

"When a woman disappears, you look for the men in her life. What about the men in her life?"

"Anne goes out with dozens of men. I don't keep track of them." Her voice was sharp, and I wondered if there was some jealousy after all.

"Could she have eloped with one of them?"

"I doubt it. Anne's quite—distrustful of men. That's natural enough, if you know Father. She's a confirmed bachelor girl, and very independent."

"Your father said she left home at fifteen. That means she's been on her own for ten years or so."

"Not exactly. She left *him* when she was fifteen, after—they had some trouble. Brand and I gave her a home until she finished high school. Then she found a job and went on her own. We tried to keep her with us, but she's very independent-minded, as I said."

"What kind of trouble did she have with your father? You said something about his corrupting her."

"Did I? I didn't mean to. He did a terrible thing to her. Don't ask me what it was." Emotion rose in her throat, thickening her voice and almost choking her, like blood from an internal hemorrhage. "Most of the men in this city are barbarians where women are concerned. It's a wretched place for a girl to try and grow up. It's like living among savages."

"As bad as that?"

"Yes. As bad as that." She cried out suddenly: "I hate this city. I know it's a dreadful thing to say, but I sometimes wish the earthquake had wiped it out entirely."

"Because your sister had trouble with your father?"

"I'm not thinking of her," she said, "or him."

I glanced at her. She was sitting rigid in the seat, her eyes almost black in the white glimmer of her face. She roused herself and leaned to touch my arm:

"You turn off here to the left. I'm sorry. I'm afraid Father upset me more than I realized."

The road spiraled off among low hills whose flanks were dotted with houses. It was a good residential suburb, where people turned their backs on small beginnings and looked to larger futures. Most of the houses were new, so new that they hadn't been assimilated to the landscape, and very modern. They had flat jutting roofs, and walls of concrete and glass skeletonized by light.

I turned up a blacktop drive at her direction and stopped the car. The house was similar to the other houses, except that there were no lights behind the expansive windows. She sat motionless, looking out at the dark low building as if it was a dangerous maze that she had to find her way through.

"This is where you live?"

"Yes. This is where I live." Her voice surrounded the words with tragic overtones. "I'm sorry. I keep saying that, don't I? But I'm afraid to go in."

"Afraid of what?"

"What are people afraid of? Death. Other people. The dark. I'm terrified of the dark. A doctor would call it nyctophobia, but knowing the name of it doesn't seem to help."

"I'll go in with you if you like."

"I would like. Very much."

I gave her my arm as we mounted the flagstone path. She held it awkwardly, pulling away, as if it embarrassed her to lean on a man. But her hip and bosom bumped me in the doorway. She took my hands in both of hers and drew me into the dark hall.

"Don't leave me now."

"I have to."

"Please don't leave me alone. I'm terribly afraid. Feel my heartbeat."

She pressed my hand to her side, so hard that my fingertips sank through the soft flesh and felt the rib cage, hammered from within by fear or something wilder. Her voice was a whisper close to my ear, so close I could feel her breath:

"You see? I am afraid. I've had to spend so many nights alone."

I kissed her lightly and disengaged myself. "You could always turn on the light."

I fumbled along the wall for the switch.

"No." She pushed my arm down. "I don't want you to see my face. I'm crying, and I'm not pretty."

"You're pretty enough for all practical purposes."

"No. Anne is the pretty one."

"I wouldn't know about Anne. I've never met her. Good night, Mrs. Church."

She answered after a pause: "Good night. I won't say I'm sorry again, but I lost my head for a minute. Brandon has to work late so often. I'll be all right when he comes home. Thank you for driving me."

"Don't mention it."

"If you do see Anne, you'll let me know right away?"

I promised her that I would, and drove back into the city.

CHAPTER **8**:   *Bougainvillea Court was guarded by* a pair of date palms which stood like unkempt sentries on either side of its entrance. When I left my car, a heavy-bodied rat crossed the sidewalk in front of me and scampered up one of the palm trunks. A pockmarked concrete cherub presided over a dry fountain in the center of the court. Each of the eight cottages surrounding it had a small front porch overgrown with purple-flowering bougainvillea. There were lights and music in most of them, but not in number three.

The door opened when I touched it. I switched on my pocket flashlight. The edge of the door was grooved and splintered around the lock. I stepped inside and closed it with my elbow. Six days missing, I thought, and sniffed instinctively for the smell of death. But all I could sense were the stale odors of life: old cigarette smoke, mixed drinks, heavy perfume, the musky indescribable odor of sex.

My light picked walls and furniture out of the darkness. There were brown Gauguin nudes on the walls and big-hatted Lautrec tarts in light wood frames; a false fireplace containing a cold gas heater, a small bookcase, spilling paperbacks, a bird's-eye maple secretary, a rattan portable bar, and a sectional davenport covered in zebra stripes, which looked both new and expensive.

The secretary was hanging open, the bolt of its flimsy lock bent out of shape. Its drawers were stuffed with papers and envelopes. The topmost envelope was addressed to Miss Anne Meyer in a masculine hand. It was empty.

A curtained archway led through a short hall to the bedroom and bathroom. The bedroom was small and feminine. The vanity and the Hollywood bed had yellow organdie skirts that matched the curtains. The closet was full of clothes—sports clothes, business suits, a couple of evening dresses, lightly scented with sachet.

It was impossible to tell if anything was missing, but there were gaps in the shoe-stand. The bed was carelessly made, and there was a rumpled depression on one side where someone had sat. A white-gold wristwatch studded with small diamonds lay on the bedside table.

There was nothing under the bed; nothing of special interest in the chest of drawers, except to underwear fetishists. Anne Meyer had spend a lot of money on underwear.

I entered the bathroom, closed the venetian blind over the little high window, and switched on the light. Nylons were strung on the towel racks over the tub. I opened the medicine cabinet above the sink. It contained the usual clutter of bottles and boxes. One cardboard box half full of blue-banded capsules was prescribed: "To be taken when needed for rest and sleep."

Shutting the mirrored door, I saw my face through the tiny snowstorm of toothpaste specks on the glass. My face was pale, my eyes narrow and hard with curiosity. I thought of the palm rat running in his shadow on the sidewalk. He lived by his wits in darkness, gnawed human leavings, listened behind walls for the sounds of danger. I liked the palm rat better when I thought of him, and myself less.

Radio music from the next cottage came loud and insistent through the closed and blinded window. *Baby, won't you please come home?* There was no toothbrush in the holder beside the sink. I went back to the vanity in the bedroom. Certain things were missing that probably should have been there: lipstick, powder, face cream, eyebrow pencil. But there were tweezers and a razor.

I returned to the front room and went through the drawers of the secretary. There was nothing personal left in them, though bills and business letters were undisturbed. A half-used checkbook showed a balance of over nineteen hundred dollars. The last stub recorded a payment of one hundred and forty-three dollars and thirty cents to Mademoiselle Finery, on October 7, eight days ago.

The pigeonholes were stuffed with receipted bills, most of them for clothes and furniture. Again nothing personal. I was ready to give up when I found a folded envelope jammed into the back of one of the pigeonholes. It had been postmarked in San Diego nearly a year before. It contained a letter written in indelible pencil on both sides of a sheet of cheap hotel stationery. The letter was signed "Tony."

I shut myself into the lighted bathroom to read it:

Dear Anne:

Maybe you are supprized to hear from me. I am supprized myself. After what you said the last time I didn't think I would want to see you again, let alone write a letter. But here I am stuck in Dago with nothing better to do this is a dreary berg since the War. I'm telling you. The ship I am supposed to meet got held up by a storm off of Baja Cal. It won't dock until tomorrow at the earliest so here I am stuck in a room in Dago for the night. I can see youre face right here in the room with me Anne. Why dont you smile at me.

I guess you think I am mentally nuts but I haven't even had a drink tonight or anything else. I was out walking before and there was plenty women I could of had. I had no interest. I had no interest in any other women since that time with you. I would marry you if you let me. I know I'm short on cash I can't complete with certain parties in the booze business but I am a loyal friend. Certain parties are the kind of fellow you

*should watch out for Anne. He is the kind of fellow
you can't trust I also heard he is going into the hole
financeanly his wifes money wont last.*

*I know you think I am a "Mexican" not good enough
for you. It isn't true Anne. My parents were pure Spanish blood no Mexican blood in my vains. I am just as
good as you are and a whiter man than "him." I would
do anything for you Anne.*

*This is not a threat. I never did threaten you. You
didn't understand when I got mad it wasn't jealousy
like you said. I was sad and worried about you. I stood
all night outside your place when "he" was there. I did
that many times. I wanted to portect you. I did that
many times. I never told you that secret did I. Dont
worry I wont tell anybody else.*

*I love you Anne. When I turn out the light I see you
in the dark shinning like a star.*

Your loyal friend,
Tony

*P.S.—Theres plenty women in this town like I said. If
I have to stay here another night I don't know what
will happen. I guess it dont matter to you one way or
the other Anne.* T.A.

I read the letter twice, straining my eyes on its small
illiterate scrawl. It was like looking through a dead man's
eyes, deciphering the smudged records of his memory.

When I opened the bathroom door, there had been a
change in the cottage. A subtler sense than hearing felt
something in the living-room, a breathing bulk solider than
the darkness. I was vulnerable with the light at my back.
The little hall and the doorless arch were like a shooting-
gallery, with me the fixed target at the end of it.

I switched off the light and moved sideways toward the

bedroom door, feeling for the doorframe with one spread hand. My other hand held the flash, ready to use as a light or as a club. I heard the rustling of the curtain in the arch six feet from me. Then the ceiling light in the hall went on with a click.

A gun was thrust past the gathered curtain at the side of the arch. It was a .45, but it was small in the hand that was holding it.

"Come out of there."

I froze in the doorway, half of my body exposed. I could feel the line between safety and danger bisecting my center.

"Out of there with your hands up." It was the sheriff's voice. "I'll give you a count of three before I fire." He began to count.

I dropped the flash in my pocket and raised my hands, stepping out of the friendly shadow. Church came through the arch. The crown of his Stetson brushed the curtain rod. He looked about seven feet tall.

"You." He came up close, pressing the muzzle of his gun into my solar plexus. "What do you think you're doing?"

"My job."

"What job is that?"

"Meyer hired me to look for his truck."

"And you thought it was concealed here, in Miss Meyer's bathroom?"

"He also hired me to look for his daughter."

He pushed the gun deeper into the hollow below my ribs, and leaned on it. "Where is she, Archer?"

I tensed myself against the gun's sharp pressure, against the sharper pressure of panic. Church's eyes were wide and blank. The muscles were ridged and dimpling around his mouth. He looked ready to kill.

"I wouldn't know where she is," I said. "I suggest you ask Kerrigan."

"What do you mean?"

"If you'll drop the tough-cop kick I'll tell you what I mean. Iron isn't good for my stomach. Neither is lead."

He pulled the gun away, looking down at it as if it was a separate entity that resisted his control. But he didn't return it to its holster.

"What about Kerrigan?"

"He crops up all over the place. When Aquista was shot, Kerrigan was the nearest citizen. The truck was loaded with Kerrigan's whisky. Now your sister-in-law turns up missing. She was Kerrigan's employee, very likely his mistress. And that's only the beginning." I was tempted to go on and tell him about the conversation I'd eavesdropped on in Sammy's Oriental Gardens. But I decided not to. It belonged to me.

Church pushed his hat back as if it constricted his thoughts. His hand stayed up, rubbing a spot on his temple: a grooved bluish-white scar, which might have been left there by a bullet-welt. He looked like a different man with his high forehead uncovered—a puzzled, sensitive man who wore the Western hat and the hard-nosed front as protective coloration. Or a man so deeply split that he didn't know himself. The gun hung down forgotten in his other hand.

When he spoke, it was in an altered voice, shallow and flat: "I've already questioned Kerrigan. He has an alibi for the shooting."

"His wife?"

"Her word is good enough for me. I've known Kate Kerrigan for a long time. I knew her father, the Judge. She's a woman I trust completely."

"A woman like that would lie for her husband."

"Maybe. She isn't lying. In any case, Kerrigan doesn't need an alibi. He's a respectable businessman."

"How respectable?"

"I'm not talking about his private life. When you've got as much to lose as Kerrigan has, you don't shoot truck-drivers on the public highway."

"Not even for seventy grand? That's a tremendous order of whisky, by the way. What does he do, take baths in it?"

"He sells it."

"In his motor court?"

"Not if I can help it. He owns a bar on the other side of town. The Golden Slipper Supper Club, he calls it."

"On Yanonali Street?"

"You get around."

"What else has he got that I don't know about—political pull?"

"I guess he has some, through his wife's connections."

I pressed the needle in a little further: "That wouldn't be influencing you on the subject of Kerrigan?"

This time it struck a nerve. A pulse jerked under the reddening scar on his temple. "You're kind of free with your questions."

"I have to take my answers where I can find them."

"Don't forget who you're talking to."

"You keep it in the forefront of my thoughts."

"You don't quite grasp the situation," he said. "I'm lean-ing over backwards. I can't promise it will last. If you want trouble, I can lock you up for breaking in the front door."

"I do a neater job than that. It was broken when I got here."

"Are you sure?"

"I'm sure. The place was burglarized, but not by an ordinary burglar. There's an expensive wristwatch on the bedroom table. A burglar would have taken it. He wouldn't have taken the other things that are missing."

"What other things?"

"Personal stuff, toothbrush and so on. I think Anne Meyer went away for the weekend and didn't come back when

she expected to. Then somebody else broke in here and
pried open her desk and removed various things, traces of
her personal life: letters, address-book, telephone numbers—"

"You had no right to barge in here," he said. "Even if
you didn't jimmy the door yourself, you're breaking the
law."

"Your wife gave me permission to search the apartment."

"What has she got to do with it?"

"Her sister is missing, she's next of kin—"

"Where did you see her?"

"I drove her home from Meyer's less than an hour ago."

"Stay away from her, do you hear me?" he said in a
rising voice. "Stay away from my house and my wife."

"Maybe you better instruct your wife to stay away from
me."

I shouldn't have said it. Anger shook and wrenched him.
His gun swung up, and the barrel clipped my chin. My
head snapped back against the wall. I heard plaster dropping down behind it. His tall figure blurred and swung
sideways like a tree falling. My arm and shoulder struck
the floor.

I got back onto my feet and wiped the blood from my
chin with the back of my hand.

"You'll probably regret this, sheriff."

"Get out of here before I do something I'll really regret."

His long face slanting forward over the gun was like
tortured bronze. His eyes were blind and empty.

I walked on remote legs to the open door. The radio
music in the next cottage had been replaced by a manic
voice asserting loudly that loneliness, fear, and unpopularity
were things of the past, abolished by chlorophyll.

CHAPTER **9**:   *Yanonali Street bent north at the city* limits to join a state highway. A pair of two-story stucco buildings stood in the angle of the roads. One was the El Recreo Pool and Shuffleboard Arcade. Men and boys brandishing cues moved in its smoky green light like heavy-footed spear-fishers walking on the floor of the sea. On the roof of the other building, a high-heeled slipper outlined in yellow bulbs hinted broadly at women and champagne gaiety. Some of the bulbs were missing.

The champagne was domestic and flat. Three girls, two weary blondes and a blue brunette, were waiting on the three end stools at the bar. Their drooping bodies straightened when I entered. They inflated their chests and opened their paint-heavy mouths in welcoming smiles. Assuming a high-minded expression, I passed them and went to the far end of the bar.

The room was shaped like a flat bottle with the narrow end in front. At the rear, beyond an empty dancing space, a deserted bandstand supported a silver-painted piano and a few music-racks like leafless metal trees. A big neurotic jukebox voice was crying out loud in an echo-chamber for love that it didn't deserve, except from tone-deaf women.

Four youths in Hawaiian-print shirts were sucking on beer bottles in one of the rear booths. Each of the four had white peroxided forelocks, as if the same lightning had blasted them all at once. They looked at me with disdain. I had ordinary hair. I wasn't atomic.

The man behind the bar wasn't atomic, either. His face resembled a tired bullfrog's. His jacket had once been white. His nostrils sighed at me when I ordered beer.

"How's business?" I said politely.

He decapitated my bottle, savagely, and set it on the

scarred formica between us. "If business improved five
hundred per cent it wouldn't even be lousy. Beer is the only
order I get any more. You on the road?"

I said I was.

"There's the life. I'd get out of here myself if I could.
Wife and family, they hold a man down." He let his shoulders slump and his jaw sag by way of illustration. "The last
year, since the big shock, this place is as dead as King Tut."

"The big shock?"

"The earthquake we had last summer. We took a beating from it, more ways than one. It scared the whole town
crapless. I guess it did some people a lot of good. This
was one wild town, brother. It ain't so wild any more, since
the big shock. A lot of leading citizens went on the wagon.
I guess they thought it was a judgment on 'em. Some of
them even started laying off of other people's wives. It
took an earthquake to do it. But oh what it did to this
business. I must of been off my rocker when I bought it."

"You own this place?"

He didn't answer. He was glaring past me at the boys
in the back booth. "Look at the class of customer I'm getting. I lose the spending trade and inherit the goof-ball
set. They nurse one piddling beer all night, just so they'll
have a place to park their drooping tails."

There was a lull in the music while the jukebox changed
its tune. One of the platinum forelocks was telling the others
how he had made a booboo with a pig. She had howitzers
like your grandma, he said, only it turned out she was
Quentin quail, a fugitive from the sixth grade. Their laughter sounded like a distant little battery of machineguns.

"Will Jo be here soon?" I asked the bartender.

He shook his head, slowly and carefully as though it
hurt him. "If it's Jo you're looking for, no dice. She ain't
coming."

"Isn't she working tonight?"

"Not tonight or any night. She quit. Which suited me fine. I was going to fire her anyway."

"I thought Don Kerrigan ran the Slipper."

"He did. Not any more. I bought it from him this morning. For which I ought to have my head examined. You a friend of Kerrigan's?"

"I've seen him around."

"Friend of Jo's?"

"I had hopes."

"You're wasting your time. She isn't coming back and even if she was you wouldn't have a chance. That mouse is all fixed up."

"With anybody in particular?"

He regarded me pawkily. "I'm a married man with four income-tax deductions. Would she confide in me?"

"If she was desperate. Does the name Tony Aquista mean anything?"

His bulging eyes seemed to retract, like a frog's eyes when it swallows. "I know Tony. He comes in, off and on."

"He won't be coming in any more. He's dead."

His face went dull and sleepy with surprise. "What happened to him?"

"Shot. On the highway south of town. He was hauling a truckload of bonded bourbon. The load was highjacked. It was billed to Kerrigan."

"How much bourbon did you say?"

"Seventy thousand dollars' worth."

"One of you is crazy. He's got no outlet for it."

"The order must have gone in several days ago. Didn't he tell you about it?"

"Maybe he did at that," he answered cautiously. "I got a very poor memory." He leaned across the bar, peering at my face from under ponderous lids. "Who are you, mister? Law?"

"A private detective. I'm investigating the job for the Meyer truck line."

"Hell, you don't think Jo had nothing to do with it?"

"That's what I want to ask her. She knew Aquista, didn't she?"

"Maybe she did. I don't know."

"You know damn well she did."

His mouth closed, and the broad planes of his face assumed a massive dignity. "Have it your way. I'm not saying nothing. The kid was no great nightingale, but she was always cheerful around the place. Why should I talk her into trouble?"

"Where can I find her?"

"She don't check back with me, paisan. And you're getting a lot of conversation out of a thirty-cent beer."

"I'll have another."

"I won't sell you another. Go back to old man Meyer and tell him to bury his head. Then you can bury yours."

I thanked him for his hospitality and slid off the bar-stool. The jukebox had a female organ now, yearning for lovers. Two of the girls from the front of the bar, the brunette and one of the blondes, were dancing on the edge of the floor. The brunette was doing the leading. I cut in on them and took the blonde.

She was pretty enough, and young, in spite of the professional glaze in her eyes. She danced expertly and eagerly, her syncopated bosom bobbing against my chest. We whirled around in a cloud of cheap perfume. That or the aftereffects of the sheriff's blow made me dizzy.

She looked up after a while and showed me a double row of fine white teeth. "I'm Jerry Mae. I love to dance."

"I used to."

"You got tired blood? You could always sit down and buy me a drink."

"I'd rather lie down."

She chose to interpret this as a pass and giggled mechanically. "You're a fast worker. I don't even know your name."

"Lew."

"Where do you hail from, Lew?"

"Los Angeles."

"I spent some time there myself. Los Angeles is a great town."

"A great town," I agreed.

Her fingertips moved on the sleeve of my jacket, assessing the probable cost of the fabric. "What do you do there, Lew?"

"Various things."

"I'd love to hear about them. Come on and sit down and buy me a drink and tell me about yourself."

"Isn't there any place we can be alone?"

She pushed me roguishly. "My, you certainly sweep a girl off her feet. If you really feel like a party, there is a room upstairs."

"Show me."

I followed her out, running the gantlet of the bartender's hostile stare. But he didn't make a move to interfere. Business was business.

A flight of wooden steps slanted up the blank stucco wall of the building. Her slim nyloned ankles climbed ahead of me. She waited for me at the upper door. Caught in the light from the roof, her face was ghastly, as if it had been stricken with yellow disease.

She led me down a corridor to the little anonymous room where her nights ended. A Hollywood bed covered with red chenille, a powder-strewn dressing-table holding an imitation-ivory radio, a sink in one corner. She closed the venetian blind over the single window and paused by the radio.

"You like music, Lew?"

"I can do without it."

There were no chairs in the room. I sat on the bed. Love
or something like it had broken its back.

She stood looking down at me with a puzzled expression.
Her eyes had the hard dismay that comes from seeing too
much for too many years and understanding too little of
it. Swallowing her doubts, she perched on my knees, letting
her skirt ride up over her thighs. The dead-white skin was
pocked with needle-marks.

"Don't you like baby?"

"I like you fine."

"Then how do you want me, honey? Peeled?"

"On ice."

"I don't get it. That's a new one, isn't it?"

"I'd rather have information than fornication." I lifted
her by the waist and set her down beside me on the bed.

She looked at me with a kind of smiling pity. "You don't
look like one of the talkers. I'm clean, if that's what's worrying you."

"Nothing's worrying me."

"I have a regular weekly examination."

"I don't doubt it."

"For Christ's sake," she said. "If all you wanted to do was
talk, we could of stayed downstairs. Now you got to pay
for the room."

"How much?"

"Five bucks. And ten for me. I charge the same for talking, that's only fair. So what do we talk about, how I got
into the racket? Or do you want to hear about the various
fellows?

"I'm interested in one fellow in particular. Tony Aquista.
Know him?"

"Sure I know him. He never went with me, though.
Personally, I wouldn't have him. I always thought he was
a little psycho."

"Is that what Jo thought, too?"

Her face hardened under its mask of paint. "I wouldn't know what Jo thought."

"Didn't she go with him?"

"Maybe she played around with him a little bit, strictly for laughs. I guess she took him home a few times."

"Recently?"

"Yeah, the last couple of weeks. The boss brought him in one night—"

"Kerrigan brought him in?"

"Yeah. He must of told her to be nice to him. I don't know of any other reason why she would bother with Tony. He hasn't even got white blood in his veins, and he's a kind of a psycho, like I said, and an awful lush. You should of seen him last time he was in. He was loaded to the gills, practically blind. Rocco had to put the dry sign on him."

"When was this?"

Her eyes rolled up in thought. "Three-four nights ago. Sunday night."

"Was Jo here?"

"Naturally. He took her home. Or she took *him* home. He wasn't navigating so good."

"What does Jo look like?"

"Why? Don't you know her?"

"Not yet."

"Seems to me you're awful interested in a girl you never saw."

"I have a reason."

"What reason?"

"It doesn't matter. Describe her."

"Well, she's a little slinky brunette, if you like the type. I was a brunette myself at one time, until I got bored with it."

"We were talking about Jo," I reminded her. "I need a complete description."

"What the hell for? I thought you wanted to *talk* to me.

Incidently, I haven't got much more time, and you owe
me fifteen."

"Does Rocco time you?"

"With a stop-watch, practically."

I took a twenty out of my wallet. It frisked away in her
hand like a little green lizard with a homing instinct for the
top of her stocking. The feel of the money seemed to en-
courage her:

"Wait a minute. If you want to know what Jo Summer
looks like, I can do better than a description."

She started for the door.

"Don't forget to come back, Jerry Mae."

"I won't."

She returned with a blue cardboard placard lettered in
gold. "This is a picture of Jo—a glamour pose. Rock just
took it out of the window yesterday."

"The Golden Slipper features gorgeous Jo Summer," the
lettering said. "Songs and sallies, three times nitely, never
a cover or minimum."

Attached to the placard was the slightly beaten photograph of a young woman. She wore a sequined black evening dress with a neckline that plunged to the waist. Her
half-restrained breasts were her most prominent features,
but it was her face that struck me: a sloe-eyed face, low-
browed under straight black bangs, with a sullen passionate
mouth. I had seen her mouth a few hours earlier, hungrily
pressed to the back of Kerrigan's hand.

I looked up at Jerry Mae. "Is she Kerrigan's girl?"

She sat on the bed beside me. "Everybody knows that.
Why do you think he gave her a job in the place?"

"What kind of a person is she? Straight or crooked?"

"How can I tell? She isn't exactly a mamma's girl, but I
can't read her mind. Half the time I can't even read my
own."

"Who are her friends?"

"I don't think she has any friends, outside of Mr. Kerrigan. How many friends does a girl need? Oh yeah, she has a grandfather, she said he was her grandfather. He came in one night last month, a few days after she started. He wanted her to pull out of here and go back home with him."

"You wouldn't know where he lives?"

"Some place out of town, I think she said in the mountains. I told her she'd be better off at home. I told her if she hung around too long in the cabarets, the wolves would tear her to pieces. I gave her the best advice I could. She's a little bit of a viper, see, and I tried to talk her out of that. She don't know what it leads to."

"What are you on, Jerry Mae? Horse?"

"We won't go into the subject of me. I'm hopeless." The corners of her heavy red mouth stretched in a bitter horizontal smile. "The kid wouldn't take my advice, so she'll have to learn it the hard way."

"Learn what?"

"You don't get any kicks in this life for free. You pay double for them afterwards, and after you run out of moxy you go on paying anyway. So now she's in a real jam, eh?"

"Could be."

"Are you a cop by any chance?"

"A private one."

"Snooping around for Mrs. Kerrigan?"

"It's a little more serious than that."

She bit her lower lip and got lipstick on her teeth. "I hope I didn't say anything to hurt the kid. She treated me kind of uppity—she thinks she's an *artiste,* and we're on different kicks—but I don't hold that against her. I was kind of uppity myself at one time. So I'm paying for it." Her hand closed on her thigh where the twenty was hidden. "How serious?"

"I won't know until I talk to her. Maybe I won't know then. Let's see, she lives in an apartment house on Yanonali Street?"

"That's right, the Cortes Apartments. If she's still there."
I got up and thanked her.

"Don't mention it. I need the money, *how* I need the money. But you had me worried there for a while. I thought I was losing it all. Which maybe I am at that." Her smile was bright and desolate. "Good night, Information. It's been the most to say the least."

"Or the least to say the most. Good night, Jerry Mae."

CHAPTER 10:   *Driving east on Yanonali Street,* I remembered the evidence case in the back of my car. It contained several hundred marijuana cigarettes, done up in packs of five. I had taken them from a pusher in South Gate and was going to turn them over to the State Bureau in Sacramento. If five were missing, the Bureau would never know the difference.

The Negro boys had vanished from the corner. I parked in front of the Cortes Apartments, opened the rear trunk, and found the small key to the evidence case on my ring. I unlocked the steel case and took out one of the little packets wrapped in butcher's paper.

The inner door of the lobby was locked. Cards bearing the tenants' names were stuck in the tarnished brass mailboxes banked along the wall. There were eighteen of them, in rows of six. Only one card was printed. Only three of the eighteen were men. Miss Jo Summer, a large immature signature in green ink, was on number seven. I pushed her button and waited.

A low voice drifted through the grille of the speaking tube. "Is that you, doll?"

"Uh-huh."

The buzzer released the door-catch. I mounted the rubber-treaded stairs into the obscurity of the building. A wall-bracket at the head of the stairs was the only light in the second-floor hallway. Someone had written a message below it with lipstick: "Chas am at Floraines see you there." My shadow climbed the wall and broke its neck on the ceiling.

Seven was the last door on the left. Its metal numeral rattled when I knocked. The door came ajar, letting out a seepage of purple light. I moved sideways out of it. The girl peered through the crack, blinking at me astigmatically. She said in her kittenish mew:

"I wasn't expecting you so soon. I was just going to take a bath."

She moved toward me, her body silhouetted in a thin rayon wrapper. One of her hands insinuated itself between my arm and my side. "A kiss for baby, Donny?"

Her wet mouth brushed the angle of my jaw. I must have tasted strange. She let out a little groan of surprise and pushed herself away from me, stood with both hands flat against the wall. Her wrapper fell open. Her body gleamed like a fish in murky water.

"Who are you? You said you were him."

"You got me wrong, Jo. Kerrigan sent me."

"He didn't say nothing to me about you."

She looked down at her breasts and gathered the wrapper across them, folding her arms. Her scarlet-taloned fingers dug into her shoulders. The kitten in her throat was scared and hissing: "Where is he? Why didn't he come himself?"

"He couldn't get away."

"Is *she* holding him up?"

"I wouldn't know. You better let me come in. He gave me something for you."

"What?"

"I'll show you inside. You have neighbors."

"Have I? I never noticed. R.K.O., come in."

She backed into the purple-lighted room, a tiny girl no taller than my shoulder, with a sleek small head and a rich body. She couldn't have been more than nineteen or twenty. I wondered how she would look when she was forty, if she lived that long.

The room was like a segment of her future waiting for her fate to overtake it. A black iron standing lamp with a red silk shade lined with blue cast its unreal light on red drapes hung from twisted iron rods, a red mohair divan piled with cheap magazines, a rug whose color and design had been trampled into indistinguishable grime. The only decoration on the yellow plaster walls was a last year's cheesecake calendar. A bored hand had given the blonde girl in the picture a mustache and goatee, and hair on her chest.

She came up to me like an eager child who had been promised a gift. "What did Donny send me?"

"This." I closed the door behind me and gave her the packet wrapped in butcher's paper.

Her fingers tore it open, scattering the brown cigarettes on the rug. She went down on her knees to retrieve them, snatching at them as if they were live worms that might wriggle away from her. She stood up with four in her hand and one in her mouth.

I flicked my lighter and lit it for her. I told myself that it was necessary, that she had the habit anyway, that police departments paid off informers with dope every day in the year. But I couldn't shake off my feeling as I watched her that I had bought a small piece of her future.

She sucked on the brown weed like a starved baby on an empty bottle. Six of her deep shuddering drags ate half of it away. She looked at what was left with growing, brightening eyes, and dragged again. Her smoky mouth wreathed itself in changing smiles. In no time at all the butt was burning her fingers.

Pressing it out in an ashtray, she put it away in an empty cigarette-case, along with the four whole reefers. She did a few dance-steps around the room, stumbling a little in her pomponed mules. Then she sat down on the red divan with her fists clenched tightly between her legs. Her eyes were huge and terribly alive, but they were turned inward, lost in the blossoming jungle of her thoughts. Her smile kept changing: girlish and silly, queenly and triumphant, whorish, feline, evil and old, and gay again and girlish.

I sat beside her. "How are you feeling, Jo?"

"I feel wonderful." Her voice came from far inside her head, barely moving her lips. "Jesus, I needed that. Thank Donny for me."

"I will if I see him. Isn't he leaving town?"

"That's right, I almost forgot, we're going away."

"Where are you going?"

"Guatemala." She said it like an incantation. "We're going to build a new life together. A beautiful new life together, with no more trouble in it, no more nastiness, no more jerks. Just him and me."

"What are you going to live on?"

"Ways and means," she said dreamily. "Donny has ways and means."

"I hope you make it."

"Why shouldn't we make it?" She gave me a black scowl. The drug had exaggerated all of her emotions, fear and hostility as well as hope.

"They're looking in his direction."

She sat up straight, pierced by anxiety. "Who? The cops?"

I nodded.

She leaned on me and took hold of my arm with both

hands and shook it. "What's the matter, isn't the protection working?"

"It takes pretty solid protection to cover murder."

Her lips curled, baring her teeth. Her eyes blazed black
in mine. "Did you say murder?"

"You heard me. A friend of yours was shot."

"What friend? I got no friends around this town."

"Doesn't Tony Aquista rate?"

Without shifting her eyes from my face, she edged away
from me, crawling on hands and buttocks into the far corner
of the divan. She said from her teeth:

"Aquista? Should I know the name? How many A's in
Aquista?"

"Don't try to kid me, Jo. He was one of your followers.
You brought him home here Sunday night."

"Who told you that? It's a lie." But she looked around
the room as if it had betrayed her. Her voice was croupy
with fear: "Did they kill Tony?"

"You ought to know. You set him up for the kill."

"No," she said. "It isn't true. I wouldn't touch a thing
like that. I'm clean."

Her gaze had returned from the interior of her dream.
She wasn't as far out of focus as I'd thought. Suspicion
flicked a bright double tongue from the black holes in the
centers of her eyes. "Tony isn't dead. You're trying to
con me."

"Would you like to pay a visit to the morgue?"

"Don didn't say anything. He would of told me if Tony
got it. It wasn't supposed to happen."

"Why would he tell you what you already knew? You
fingered Tony, didn't you?"

"I did not. I didn't even set eyes on him since last Sunday night. I've been home here all day today." She rose
and stood over me, her face drawn and jaundiced. "Is
somebody trying to frame me? Who are you, anyway?"

"A friend of Don's. I talked to him tonight."

"Don wouldn't do that to me. Is he arrested?"

"Not yet."

"Are you sluff?"

"Oh sure," I said. "That's why I brought you those reefers."

"Where did Don get them?" Her black gaze slanted down at me from under her broad low brow.

"From Bozey. Don couldn't bring them himself, so he sent me."

"Funny he never mentioned you."

"He doesn't tell you everything."

"No. I guess he doesn't."

She crossed the room to the venetian-blinded window and ran her fingers idly down the slats. She returned with dragging feet and made herself small in the corner of the divan, hugging her knees to her breast.

"I don't know what's going on," she said. "You tell me Tony's dead and Don's been stringing me. Why should I listen to you?"

"I'm telling the truth."

"Are you supposed to be in on the deal?"

"I thought I was. But it looks as if he's been stringing both of us. The way he laid the blueprint out for me, you were the one that was going to finger Tony."

"That was the original plan," she said. "I was supposed to flag him down. No shooting, understand—I wouldn't go for that. Just stop the truck on the road and let the others take over."

"Don and Bozey?"

"Yeah. Only they changed the plan. Don didn't want me sticking my neck out, see." She stroked her round smooth neck, unconsciously. "And then something came up—something that Tony told me Sunday night. He was drunk when he told me, I didn't believe it at the time. He was always full of blowtop tales about her. But Don believed it when I told him."

"What did you tell him?"

"This tale about Anne Meyer."

"Try it on me."

She pinched the skin of her throat between thumb and forefinger and looked at me sideways. "You ask an awful lot of questions. How do I know you're not a cop? How do I know those reefers weren't a come-on?"

I stood up, feigning anger, and moved to the door. "Have it your way, sister. I can take so much, but when you call me sluff—"

She followed me. "Wait a sec. You don't have to flip your lid. Okay, you're a friend of Don's, you're in on the deal. What are you doing now?"

"I'm getting out. I don't like the smell of it."

"Do you have a car?"

"It's outside."

"Will you drive me some place?"

"If you say so. Where?"

"I don't know where. But I'm not going to sit here and wait to be picked off." She went to an inner door and turned with her hand on the knob. "I'll shower and put some clothes on. It won't take a minute." Her smile went on and off like an electric sign.

I waited for fifteen minutes, lulled by the splattering rush of the shower behind the wall. I smoked an old-fashioned cigarette made of tobacco and leafed through the "romance" magazines on the divan. I Was a Love Decoy. My Lost Weekend. Do Men Have Forbidden Desires? I Was an Old Man's Plaything. The cover girls all looked like Jo, in one way or another. She was legion.

It hit me finally that her shower-bath had lasted much too long. I walked into her bedroom without knocking. The bureau drawers were hanging open, empty except for a few soiled clothes. I opened the bathroom door. The shower was running full force into the bathtub, but there was no girl under it.

I went through the dark kitchen, out the back door, down a flight of wooden steps into a walled alley. A little light filtered down through the porous sky. It showed me a fat old Negro wedged in a sitting position between two garbage cans against the wall. With his head hanging sideways and his legs spraddled, he looked like a huge black baby left on the world's doorstep. I shook him and smelled the rotgut and let him sleep.

I went toward the mouth of the alley, a high pale rectangle filled with diluted light from the corner streetlamp. A man's figure entered its frame. Wide-shouldered and narrow-hipped in a leather windbreaker, he moved with a tomcat's grace and silence. I caught a glimpse of his face. It was young and pale. Dark red hair hung down over his temples in lank wings. He pushed it back with one hand. His other hand was hidden under the windbreaker. The wall's shadow fell across him.

"Did you happen to see a girl come out of here?"

"What girl?"

"A little brunette. She's probably carrying a suitcase."

"Yeah. I saw her."

He moved along the wall toward me, so close that I could see his eyes and the frightened savage lostness in them.

"Which way did she go?"

"That depends on what you want from her. What do you want from her?"

His voice was quiet and calm, but I could sense the one-track fury behind it. He was one of the dangerous boys, born dry behind the ears and weaned on fury and grief.

"You wouldn't be Bozey?"

He didn't answer in words. His fist came out from under

the windbreaker, wearing something bright, and smashed at the side of my head.

My legs forgot about me. I sat on the asphalt against the wall and looked up at his armed right fist, a shining steel hub on which the night revolved. His face leaned over me, stark and glazed with hatred.

"Bow down, God damn you, sluff. I'm Bozey all right. Bow down and kiss my feet."

His bright fist drove downward at my face. I slipped the punch somehow and heard metal jar on stone. I tried to get to my feet. But my legs were made of old rope and worn-out rubber. The third blow found me, and the night revolved more quickly, like dirty water going down a drain.

When I came to, I was in my car, trying to turn the trunk key in the ignition. The street was deserted, and that was just as well. I drove like a drunk for a couple of blocks, weaving from curb to curb. Then my vision cleared and steadied.

Crossing the main street, I saw my bleeding face in the mirror over the windshield. It looked curiously lopsided. I glanced at my wristwatch to see what time it was. My wrist was bare. I shook myself down and found that my wallet was missing. But my .38 was still in the glove compartment. I transferred it to the side pocket of my jacket.

CHAPTER 11:   *Kerrigan's house stood on a slope* in the northeastern part of the city. I U-turned in the intersection above it and parked in the slanting street. It was a street of elderly homes with spacious lawns, shadowed by trees and well-clipped shrubbery. Seen from above, the tiled roofs floated in a dark green cascade of foliage. It was getting late, and most of the houses were dark. Kerrigan's wasn't. The red Ford convertible was standing in front of it.

I left the sidewalk, waded through dew-dense grass to the side of the next house, and stepped over a low field-stone wall into Kerrigan's yard. The terraced lawn was splashed with light from the windows. There was a rumor of voices inside the house. The windows were too high for me to see through. I moved along the wall toward the front. There were two voices, a man's and a woman's. The man's voice was pitched almost as high as the woman's.

The front veranda was a deep railed platform partly shaded with split-bamboo screening. It was further shielded from the street by a great old monkey-puzzle tree that grew in front of it. I jumped for the railing, caught it, pulled myself up and over.

From where I stood in the corner of the veranda against the wall, I couldn't see into the house. Moving across the light from the window, I reached the shelter of a green canvas glider. By pulling aside the canvas shade behind the swinging seat, I could see the interior of the room without being seen.

It was a beautiful room, white-carpeted and filled with the suave and fragile curves of eighteenth-century furniture. The airy white ceiling was supported on Ionic capitals, repeated in the pilastered marble mantel. Someone with Europe on his mind had tried to trap a dream of civilization in the room, and almost succeeded. Its present occupants were standing in front of the fireplace, telling each other that the dream was stone dead.

The woman's back was to me, straight and tense. A pearl collar gleamed coldly on her neck, under the yellow hair. "What I had is gone," she said, "so you're running out. I always knew you would."

"You always knew, eh?" Kerrigan stood facing her, leaning negligently against the mantel. One hand was in his pocket, the other held a short briar pipe. It was an actorish pose.

"Yes. I've known for a long time. For four or five years at least, since you took up with the Meyer woman."

"That was over long ago."

"So you let me believe. But you've never been honest with me."

"I've tried. You want me to level with you? You want the honest truth?"

"You're not capable of telling it, Don. You're a helpless liar. You lied to me before we were married, about your resources, your prospects. Your alleged love for me." Her voice broke scornfully. "Your entire life with me has been a lie. You haven't even given me common fidelity."

"Prove it."

"I don't have to. I know. You think you fooled me with your childish excuses, when you came home to my house with your clothes disarranged, your mouth red—"

"Wait a minute." He pointed the stem of his pipe like a gun at her head. "Did you hear yourself, Kate? You know what you just said. *Your* house, you called it. Not our house. Yours. And you wonder why I feel like an interloper."

"Because you are one," she said. "You are an interloper. My grandfather built this house for my grandmother. They left it to my father. My father left it to me. It's mine. The house is one thing you'll never get your hands on."

"Who wants it?"

"You do, Don. It was only the other day you were trying to persuade me to sell it and give you the money."

"So I was." He shrugged his shoulders, smiling crookedly. "Well, it's too late now. You can keep your house and live in it by yourself. I never really lived in this house. I lived in the doghouse behind it, and you put me there. Keep the doghouse, too. You'll need it for your next husband."

"Would I be likely to marry again, after my experience with you?"

"It wasn't as bad as that, now, Kate. You're no tragic figure, don't go dreaming you are. I admit I wasn't in love with you when we got married. Hear me admitting it? I married you for your money. Is that such a terrible crime? Your hotshot friends in Santa Barbara do it every day. Hell, I thought I was doing you a good turn."

"Thank you for your gracious kindness—"

"No, listen to me for a change." His voice deepened, and he forgot his pose. "You were all by yourself. Your parents were dead. Your lover got himself killed in the war—"

"Talley wasn't my *lover.*"

"That I can believe. Listen to me. You needed a man more than you needed money. Okay. I elected myself to fill the bill. I didn't make it, but you'll never know how hard I tried. I went into this thing to make it work, on a fifty-fifty basis. I couldn't make it work. I had no chance to. You never trusted me. You never even liked me."

"I loved you, though." She turned away from him. Her hands went to her breasts and held them as if they ached.

"You thought you loved me, I'll give you that much. Maybe you loved me in your head. Only what good is love in the head? It's just a word. You're still a virgin as far as I'm concerned. Did you know that, Kate? It's been chilly work, trying to be your husband. You never made me feel like a man. Not once."

Her face was drawn sharp over the harsh bones. She fingered the collar of pearls at her throat. "I'm not a magician," she said.

He raised his eyes to the blank patrician ceiling. "What's the use?"

"No use. It's over and done with, if there ever was anything there. It only confirmed what I knew when I found you packing your bags. I wasn't even surprised. I realized what was coming a month ago."

"Last time it was five years."

"Yes, but I kept hoping. When you broke off with Anne Meyer, or claimed you did, I thought perhaps our marriage had a chance. I was a fool to allow myself any hope, wasn't I? I saw what a fool I was last month—the day I met you on the grounds of the Inn with that girl on your arm. And you pretended not to know me, Don. You wouldn't look at me. You kept looking at her."

"I don't know what you mean," he said without conviction. "I never was at the Inn with any girl."

"Of course not." She turned on him suddenly, clenching her hands. "Does she make you feel like a man, that little tar-haired creature? Does she build you up with flattery and give you delusions of grandeur and renew your youth for you?"

"Leave her out of this."

"Why should I? Is she so sacred? Aren't you going away with her? Isn't that the big project for tonight?"

"You're crazy."

"Am I? You're going away, aren't you? You're not the kind of man who goes by himself. You need a woman along to keep your ego wrapped in cotton batting. I don't know what woman, I don't care. For all I know, you've taken up with Anne Meyer again. Or maybe you've kept her on the string all along."

"Now you're really getting crazy."

"Am I? You gave her the keys to the lodge last Friday. I heard her thank you for them. I wouldn't be surprised if she was up at the lake now, waiting for you to join her."

"Don't be ridiculous. I told you that was over. I don't know where she is any more than you do."

"She spent the weekend at Lake Perdida. Didn't she?"

"All right. I told her she could have the lodge for the weekend. We weren't using it. It was standing empty. I gave her the keys. Does that make me a criminal?"

"You're going there now," she said accusingly.

"I am not. Anne isn't there anyway. I drove up to the lake on Monday to look for her, and she was gone."

"Gone where?"

"I don't know. Can you get that through your head? I don't know." The subject seemed to disturb him. "You'd think I was running a harem."

"I wouldn't be surprised if you were. You don't even know you exist unless a woman whispers it in your ear. Any woman."

"Not any woman. Not you." His voice was soft with malice.

"No," she said. "Not me. I don't know who it is this time. But I can tell you one thing, it won't last. It won't last seven *months*."

"That's what you think."

"I know it. You run through sex the way you run through money. They're the same thing to you, something to soothe your itch and make you forget what a dismal loss you are."

"You know it all, eh? All you know is what you read in your damn books. I'll give you a little piece of information, Kate. This wouldn't have happened if you'd given me a break when I asked you for it."

"I've given you a lot of breaks, as you call them." But she sounded a little defensive, for the first time. The lines of her back and shoulders softened, and she seemed to lean toward him. "Don? You're in real difficulty, aren't you? Is it really serious this time?"

"You'll never know."

"Couldn't we be honest with each other, just this once? I'll do what I can to help."

"You will, eh?"

"Yes. Even if it did mean giving up the house. If that's what you really need."

"I don't need anything that you have," he said.

She recoiled as if from a blow. After a while she repeated his name. "Don. Why did Brand Church come here to-night?"

"Routine investigation."

"It didn't sound like that to me."

"Were you eavesdroping?" He walked toward her.

"Certainly not. I couldn't help overhearing your voices. You had a dreadful scene with him."

"Forget it."

"Don, was it about the murder?"

"I said forget it." His fingers curled around the pipe and clenched, snapping the amber stem. His voice rose: "Forget all about me. I'm a dismal loss as you said. It's not all my fault. There's something wrong with this town, too. At least it wasn't for me. And I had bad luck. If the government had gone through with the reopening of the Marine Base, the court would be coining money. I'd be rolling in it."

She answered harshly, as if she had given him up: "You'd find a way to lose it. But blame the government if it makes you feel better. Blame me and the town and the government."

He shook his broken pipe at her. "A man can take so much. I've had my bellyful. I'm getting out."

He started across the room toward the door. His wife called after him: "You don't fool me. You've been planning this for weeks. You just don't have the manhood to admit it."

He stopped in his tracks. "Since when have you been interested in manhood? It's the last thing that would appeal to you."

"I've never been tested."

"Take a look at me, then. Make it a good one. It will be your last."

He thrust his face toward her, breathing heavily through distended nostrils. She laughed. It sounded like something delicate and brittle breaking inside of her.

"Is this what manhood looks like? Is this how it talks? Is this how a husband speaks to a wife?"

"What wife?" he said. "I don't see any wife." Kerrigan shaded his eyes with one hand and scanned the dissolving horizons of the room. Then turned, grinding his heel in the white carpet, and wrenched the door open. I heard his angry feet stamp up the stairs.

Kate Kerrigan drifted to the mantel and laid her head and her arm along its line. Her hair fell like ungathered sheaves across her face. I looked away from her.

The monkey-puzzle tree was sharply conventionalized against the red city sky. Below it Las Cruces lay tangled in its lights. The thickest, brightest cord in the net of lights was the yellow-lit freeway that carried the highway. The highballing trucks and cars, from the distance at which I sat, were like children's toys pushed without purpose across the face of midnight.

At the other end of the veranda a door opened. I pulled my legs up out of sight. Kerrigan stepped out, his shoulders bowed by a heavy leather suitcase in each hand.

"This is for good?" she said behind him.

"That's for sure. I'm taking my own car, incidentally. And nothing else except my clothes."

"Of course you're leaving your debts."

"The businesses ought to cover them. If they don't it's just too bad."

She appeared in the lighted doorway, a pale figure holding out one tentative hand. "Where are you going, Don?"

He said with his back to her: "You'll never know."

"It's strange that you're able to walk away like this. Even you."

"It's better than being carried out on a litter," he said over his shoulder. "So long, Kate. Don't make trouble for me. If you do, you'll get double trouble. I promise."

She watched him go down the steps and along the walk to the street, where his car was parked. Her fingers clutched at her throat. They tore the pearl collar. The beads rattled like hail on the tiles.

CHAPTER 12:   *His double red taillight dimin-*ished down the slope, flashed at a boulevard stop, and disappeared. When I reached the boulevard, his car was a long block away, headed south toward the suburbs. I kept the block's distance between us as far as the wye at the city limits. Then I closed in on him, cutting in and out through the highway traffic, past all-night businesses whose signs were like a neon postscript scribbled in the dirty margin of the city.

We were only a couple of miles from his motor court, and I thought that he was on his way there. Instead, he pulled out of the southward stream of traffic and turned in on the asphalt apron of a drive-in restaurant. Its parking space held two cut-down jalopies occupied by mugging couples, and a blue Buick coupe with battered fenders. As I went by, I saw Kerrigan draw up beside the Buick.

Next door to the drive-in stood a dark and unattended service station. I stopped beside its gas pumps. From where I sat, I could see the entrance to the drive-in and one glass wall of the building. A couple of car-hops, wan-looking under blue light, were talking behind the glass to a white-hatted short-order cook. Through the glass of the far wall, Kerrigan's red Ford and the Buick coupe were dimly visible.

Kerrigan was standing between the two cars, talking to someone in the Buick. Its occupant, whose face was hidden from me, held out a package wrapped in dirty paper or newsprint. Kerrigan stuffed the package under his coat and returned to his car. The Buick's headlights went on. It backed and turned toward the entrance. I caught a glimpse of a fur-collared leather jacket, a pale hard face framed in lank red hair. Bozey. A jet of adrenaline went through me. I followed him south out of town.

As the Buick fled into the dark perspective of the country, my excitement rose with my speed. I passed Kerrigan's motor court at seventy. The speedometer climbed to seventy-five and held there. The Buick stayed in sight.

A few miles farther on, it slowed and seemed to hesitate, turned off the highway to the right. Its headlights swept a side road lined with cyclone fence. Then they were cut. I passed the intersection, slowing gradually, and saw its lightless shape crawling blind along the blacktop.

I braked hard, hit the dirt, cut my own lights and U-turned. When I rolled slowly back to the intersection, the Buick was out of sight and out of hearing. I turned down the blacktop after it and drove for nearly half a mile without lights.

The night was starless and moonless. A diffused radiance in the sky was enough to give me my bearings. The road ran straight as a yardstick between the high wire fences on either side. The sloping field to my left was gashed and plowed by erosion like a landscape on the dark side of the moon. The hangars of the disused airbase loomed on the other side. Around them concrete runways lay like fallen tombstones in the wild grass.

There was a break in the fence. I stopped in the ditch beyond it, and twirled the chamber of my .38 special to make sure that it was fully loaded. It was. I got out of the car. Except for the rusty sighing of cicadas, the night was very still. My footsteps made distinct sounds in the grass. A double wire gate about thirty feet wide stood open in the fence. Its padlock bar had been filed through. I felt the sharp edges with my fingers. A concrete road ran through the gate and merged with one of the runways. The door of the nearest hangar yawned open. The Buick was standing beside it.

I started toward it, across two hundred yards of open concrete. There was no other movement anywhere under the heavy sky. I felt small and expendable. The revolver in my hand was cold comfort. The high whistling whine of a starting Diesel penetrated the silence. Headlights flared inside the cavelike hangar. I broke into a run, hoping to get there before the motor warmed. But it must have been primed with gasoline. The truck rolled out of the building, pulling its huge aluminum semi-trailer. Its headlights swung toward me. A white face gleamed in the darkness of the cab.

As the truck bore down on me, I took careful aim at the lower left-hand corner of the windshield and fired twice. Cracks spiderwebbed the glass, but it didn't shatter. Without swerving or slackening, the truck roared directly at me.

When it was almost on top of me, I stepped to one side and ran away from it. Its multiple tires growled in my ear. Something tugged at my trouser leg and spun me. I got a tight grip on air and hit the concrete like a sack of sand. Slid down its deadend street to the rough edge of unconsciousness and went over.

It was a long fall straight down through the darkness of my head. I was a middle-aging space cadet lost between galaxies and out of gas. With infinite skill and cunning I put a grain of salt on the tail of a comet and rode it back to the solar system. My back and shoulder were burned raw from the sliding fall. But it was nice to be home.

I sat up and looked around. There was nothing to see

except the bare concrete, the open hangar, the abandoned coupe beside it. From somewhere and everywhere the cicadas chided me: you should have waited and followed, hated and swallowed, waited and followed. I got to my feet and searched for my gun and found it. It was a long walk back to my car.

I backed in through the open gate and drove to the front of the hangar. My headlights stabbed the darkness of its interior, shining on a pool of oil where the truck had stood. There was nothing else in the place but an empty Coke-bottle, years' accumulation of dust drifted along the walls, some spatters of aluminum paint on the concrete-slab floor. I touched one metallic droplet with my finger. It wasn't quite dry.

I went outside to the Buick. It was a fairly new car, but driven to pieces. California plates. No registration card. Several brown cigarette butts squashed on the rubber floor-mat. I sniffed them. Marijuana. A road map of the South-western states was jammed behind the front-seat cushion. I took it along and drove back to the highway.

The blacktop crossed it and plunged into the foothills in the distance. I sat at the intersection, my motor idling, and looked at the black mountainous horizon. It was a jagged graph of high hopes, repeated disasters.

There was a black and white sign on the far side of the highway: LAS CRUCES PASS. I tried to put myself in Bozey's place. If he had turned right and south, he'd be sure to hit a roadblock on the borders of the county. Northward, the highway would lead him back into town. The pass road seemed most likely, and I took it.

Four or five miles from the intersection, where the road twisted high and narrow among the foothills, I came around a hairpin curve and saw a pulsating red light. A black car was parked diagonally across the road. I braked to a stop in time. It was the sheriff's Mercury.

He came forward, carrying a red flashlight in his left hand, a carbine in the crook of his other arm.

"Pull off the road and get out. Keep your hands in sight." Then the flashlight beam found my face. "So it's you again."

I sat perfectly still under the eye of the carbine, the flashlight's red stare. "It's also you again. Have you seen the truck?"

"What truck?"

"Meyer's semi-trailer."

"Would I be sitting up here if I had seen it?" His voice was impatient, but the anger that had shaken him earlier had passed through him and left no other trace.

"How long have you been here, sheriff?"

"Over an hour."

"What time is it now?"

"One o'clock, a few minutes after. Is there anything else you'd like to know? What I had for supper, for intance?"

"That sounds interesting."

"I didn't get to eat any supper." He leaned in at the window to look at me. The reflection of the flashlight lent his face an unnatural rosiness. "Who's been clobbering you?"

"You're very solicitous all of a sudden. It moves me deeply."

"Cut the vaudeville. And answer my question."

"Since you put it so charmingly. I took a fall." I told him where and how. "This redhead had the truck stashed in an empty hangar at the airbase. He blanked out Meyer's signs with aluminum paint and waited for the heat to die down. Less than an hour ago, Kerrigan met him at the Steakburger drive-in and gave him the go-ahead."

"You know this?"

"I saw them together. The redhead—his name is Bozey—handed Kerrigan a paper package of something, probably something long and green. Kerrigan's payoff."

"Payoff for what?"

"For setting up the truck, and arranging the getaway."

"How would Kerrigan do that?"

I didn't answer. We looked at each other in silence. The mountains rose behind him in the distance like a surf of stone beating soundlessly on an iron sky. Shadowed by his hatbrim, his face was as inscrutable as the sky.

"Aren't you a little hipped on this Kerrigan business?" he said. "I don't like the bastard, either. But that doesn't mean he's involved with a gang of highjackers."

"The facts all point in his direction. I've given you some of them. There are others. He ordered a load of whisky that he had no use for."

"How do you know that?"

"He sold the Slipper this morning. He's leaving his wife for another woman, and he needs ready cash, a lot of it."

"Who's the other woman?"

"Not your sister-in-law, if that's what's worrying you. She seems to be out of it. The girl's name is Jo Summer, and she had a singing engagement at the Slipper. The last couple of weeks she's been playing up to Aquista, apparently getting set to finger him. You've got enough evidence there to book them—"

"Evidence? I've got your story."

"Check it. Go over the ground yourself. Round up the suspects before they leave the county."

"You seem to be instructing me in my duties."

"It seems to be necessary."

"Don't let that paranoid streak run away with you. I can sympathize with your feelings, after the beating you took. But there are worse things than a beating. So I wouldn't press too hard, Archer."

"That could be a threat."

"It could be, but it isn't. It wouldn't be good for me if

you got hurt in my territory—badly hurt. And it wouldn't be good for you. You can't see much and you can't do much on the bottom of an irrigation ditch with a bullet in your head."

I had my hand on the revolver in my pocket. "Is a carbine bullet what you had in mind?"

Church fingered the stock of his carbine. His face was impassive, almost dreamy. A light wind from the mountains probed my clothes and chilled me. The moral chill went deeper. He said:

"You didn't catch my meaning, I'm afraid. I don't want anything to happen to you. If you'll take my advice, you'll check in at the hospital and get yourself patched up and treat yourself to a rest. That ought to be clear enough."

"Crystal clear. I lay off Kerrigan and his gentle friends."

"You lay off, period. I can't assume responsibility for you if you keep on throwing your weight around. Good night."

He stepped back to let me turn. The last I saw of him, he was standing in the road beside his car, a lonely silhouette.

CHAPTER **13**: *I drove back down the pass road* and turned toward the city. The glow of its lights was paler, as if the fires that consumed it were burning out. A few late trucks went by toward the south, their headlights long white fingers reaching for morning. None of them was a rig I had seen before. Bozey would be out of the county by this time, headed east or south. Kerrigan would be on his way to Mexico.

I was wrong about Kerrigan. His red convertible was standing on the gravel apron in front of his motor court. The engine was idling, and its blue-gray exhaust puffed and plumed on the air.

I parked on the shoulder of the highway and walked back to the convertible. It was empty. Switching off the ignition, I dropped the keys in my pocket and took my gun out. All but one of the cottages in the court were dark, but there was light in the main building. It leaked through a side window and glazed the green surface of the small oval swimming-pool. I walked around the pool to the rear of the building. The water looked deep and cold.

The light was in the office. Its back door was partly open, and I looked in. The room was newly furnished with a couple of chromium chairs, a metal desk with a black composition top, fluorescent fixtures in the ceiling. Kerrigan was prone between the desk and a small safe, which was open. The back of Kerrigan's head was open too. In the blank efficient light, I could see the color of his brains.

The cork floor around his head was soaked with blood. I lifted his head by the short hair and saw where the bullet had entered, between the eyes. It looked like a medium-caliber hole, probably .38. The gray triangular eyes were fixed in eternal surprise. I turned them back to the floor and went through his pockets, quickly. A siren in the distance was whirling a thin loop of sound over the rooftops.

Kerrigan had no wallet, no money in any form. There was no trace of the package Bozey had handed him, either in his clothes or in the safe. I pulled out the contents of the safe: bills and canceled checks, the current ledger for the motor court. It had been losing money.

Somewhere on the other side of the court an engine turned over, coughed, and died. The starter whined again, insistently. I left the dead man and followed the broken thread of sound outside. It came from one of the doorless carports fronting on the alley behind the cottages.

The whining motor caught and turned over, roaring. I started to run toward the mouth of the alley, my leather soles clattering and sliding on the tiles around the pool.

A small sports car with the top down backed out of the
carport behind the lighted cottage, paused with a squeak
of rubber, and shot toward the highway. Jo Summer's
face was darkly intent behind the windshield.

I raised my gun. "Stop. I'll fire."

Then something heavy and hard and grunting struck my
legs from behind. I went down at the side of the alley. The
little car swerved around me, flicking gravel into my face.
A pair of knees hit the small of my back like piledrivers.
An arm circled my neck in a stranglehold, and another
arm reached for my gun.

I held onto the gun, and used it to hammer the elbow
bent around my throat. The man on my back growled with
pain. His grip relaxed. Using his arm as a lever, I got my
shoulder under his weight. He must have weighed two
hundred. My muscles creaked as I rose to my knees. I
flipped him forward over my head and pinned him on his
back, one arm under his neck, the other between his writh-
ing legs.

The man's legs were encased in black leather, and I didn't
like the color of his breeches. They seemed to be olive-
drab in the chancy light. They looked like part of the
uniform of the sheriff's department. A choked voice said
something about arrest into my armpit.

I let him go, but I picked up my gun and held it on him
as he got to his feet. It was Deputy Braga, Tony Aquista's
cousin. His teeth were a bright gash in his Indian face,
and his breath hissed out between them like escaping
steam.

"Give me that gun."

"I think it's safer with me, Braga."

His quick obsidian eyes went from the gun to my face
and back again. "Hand it over. I saw you pull it on the
girl."

"I was trying to stop her. She's one of the highjacking

mob. That was a brilliant tactic of yours, letting her get away."

"Listen, you smart-cracking L.A. bastard—"

He took a step toward me. I moved the gun, and it inhibited him.

"Listen to me. She's Kerrigan's girl, and Kerrigan is on the floor of his office with his brains blown out."

"Is that the shot that was heard? Are you the one that reported it?"

"No."

His brown face was wooden with thought. "There's too damn many coincidences here. You make a habit of finding murder victims in pairs?"

"I was tailing Kerrigan. If you want to know why, ask the sheriff. I laid it out for him a few minutes ago."

"The hell you did. He's way up in the pass, manning a roadblock."

"That's where I talked to him. Speaking of coincidences, does Church make a habit of doing his own detail work?"

"I'll ask the questions." He took another step toward my gun, leaning on its menace like a man walking into a strong wind. "I'm telling you for the last time. Drop the gun."

"Sorry, Braga. I need it. I'm going after the girl."

"You're staying here."

He crouched and went for his hip. I had the choice of shooting him or letting him shoot me. Or swinging on him with everything I had left, on the chance of finding the point of his outthrust chin. I found it. He lay down on his side, very still, in fetal position.

I heard a click behind me. The door of the lighted cottage opened. A wispy-haired youth in red pajamas came toward me, walking like a sleepwalker. I stepped in front of Braga and went to meet him.

"Who are you?"

"Allister Gunnison. Junior." He sounded like a butler

announcing his own arrival at a funeral. "Are you the officer I called? I'm sure I heard a shot."

"What time?"

"I believe it was about a quarter after one. I happened to look at my traveling clock when the noise awakened me. Then I heard running footsteps."

"Coming in this direction, toward the alley?"

"No, I believe they went toward the highway, over on the other side of the court."

"Man's or woman's?"

"I really couldn't say. There was no one in sight by the time I got outside. After I called you on the public telephone, I came back to my cottage and took a luminol. I'm afraid I must have gone into shock or something—I just came out of it now. You see, I'm terribly high-strung, my nerves can't endure excitement."

"You're not the only one. Does the sports car belong to you?"

"The MG? Yes, it does."

"You shouldn't leave the keys in it. It's been stolen."

"Oh, my," he said, "how dreadful. Mother will be fearfully upset. And I have to face her in Pasadena tomorrow. You simply must get it back for me, officer."

His myopic eyes focused on me for the first time, took in my face, the wreckage of my clothes. "You're not—are you a policeman?" His hand went to his mouth.

"A special agent from Washington," I said. "We've had our eye on you for wearing red pajamas. Watch it, Gunnison."

I left him munching his knuckles in wild surmise. Braga was twitching when I passed him. I ran the rest of the way to my car. At least I went through the motions of running, and didn't fall on my face.

Before I reached the city limits, I realized the hopelessness of the chase. Jo had a long head start, and she

wouldn't be going back to any of the places she'd been.
I went to see Mrs. Kerrigan instead.

CHAPTER 14:   *There was music in the house*
behind the monkey-puzzle tree: a nervous dialogue of
piano and strings. Pity me, the piano said. We pity you,
said the strings. The music was switched off when I
knocked on the door. Mrs. Kerrigan opened it on a chain.

"Who is it?"

"Archer."

Her voice and her look were vague. "Oh yes, I remember—at the motor court."

"I just came from there. Your husband has had an accident."

"An automobile accident?"

"A shooting accident."

"Don? Is he seriously hurt?"

"Very seriously. May I come in?"

She fumbled with the chain, finally got it unhooked,
and stood back to let me enter. She had on a blue serge
bathrobe, severely cut, with white piping. Below it, her
slender legs were sheathed in nylon, and she was wearing
shoes.

"I couldn't sleep," she said. "I believe I had a premonition of something wrong. I've been sitting here listening
to the Bartók. It's very much like listening to the sound
of my own thoughts—two-o'clock-in-the-morning thoughts."

She closed the door with a decisive click and made an
effort to pull herself together. Her eyes were slightly
puffed, by tears or insomnia. They rested on my face.

"You've been injured, too, Mr. Archer."

"I don't matter at the moment. I'll survive."

"How badly is Don hurt?"

"As badly as possible."

"I should go to him, shouldn't I?" She went to the foot of the staircase, then turned with her hand on the newel post. "Do you mean that he is dead?"

"He was murdered, Mrs. Kerrigan. I wouldn't go there now if I were you. They'll be coming here."

"They?"

"The police, the sheriff's men. They'll have some questions to ask you. So have I."

She moved uncertainly through the door to the living-room and leaned on the white silk arm of the chesterfield, teetering a little like a slender tree in gusts of wind. She stroked her forehead with her fingertips. I could see the fine blue veins in her wrist.

"Give me a moment, won't you? That concerto is still running in my head. I shouldn't have put it on when I was feeling so vulnerable. I feel as if I've been widowed twice on the same night." She raised her head. "How was he killed? Did you say he was shot?"

"In his office at the motor court, no more than an hour ago."

"And I'm a suspect, is that what I'm to understand?"

"Not with me."

"Why not?"

"Let's say I like your face."

"I don't," she said with a child's seriousness. "I don't like my face. You must have a better reason than that."

"All right. *Did* you shoot him?"

"No." She went on in a harsher, stronger voice: "But don't mistake what I'm feeling for any kind of grief. It's simply—confusion. I don't know what to feel. I haven't much feeling left, actually. And I can't say I'm sorry that it was done. Don wasn't a good man. Which was fair enough, I suppose. I'm not a good woman."

"I wouldn't talk like that to the police. The police mind

likes simple, obvious patterns, and they're likely to tab
you as the primary suspect. You're going to need an alibi
in any case. Do you have one?"

"For when?"

"The last hour or so."

"I've simply been here at home."

"Nobody with you?"

"No. I've been listening to records for an hour or more.
Before that, I must have spent an hour picking up my
beads. I spilled them on the porch. When I had them all
picked up, I took them and threw them away. Wasn't
that an insane thing to do?" Her fingers returned to her
temples, which were hollow and smooth and delicate as
shell. "Don used to tell me I was insane. Do you suppose
he was right?"

"I think you're a good woman who has gone through a
lot of suffering. I'm sorry you have to go through more."

I touched her blue serge shoulder. It didn't yield to my
pressure. She sat rigid, blinking back tears.

"Don't be sympathetic, I'm not used to sympathy. I'd
almost rather be accused of killing him. I'd probably feel
less empty if I had."

"What if you had? Would you deny it?"

"I don't believe I would," she said slowly. "Honesty is
one virtue I have left. Probably the only one."

"Why cut yourself down so small?"

"The cutting down was done for me, by an expert. Don
could be quite a sadist when the spirit moved him. The
spirit often moved him." She closed her eyes tightly for
a second. "I was cruel, too. It wasn't all one-sided. The
truth is, when he left this house tonight—Don left me
tonight, Mr. Archer, and I thought of killing him then.
The actual picture crossed my mind. I could see myself
very plainly, following him down to the street and shooting him in the back. I might have done it, too, if I'd had

a gun. But it would have been perfectly pointless, wouldn't it?" Her eyes came up like dark blue lights. "Who did kill him, do you know?"

"It's hard to say. The Summer girl was at the scene—"

"That dirty-eyed little brunette of his?"

I nodded. "She got away in a stolen car. It doesn't prove that she shot him, though."

"That would be an irony now, if she did. The whole situation is ironic. Don was going away to start a new life, as he called it. *Vita nuova.*" Her mouth curled over the words.

"It isn't as ironic as it looks. Your husband was neck-deep in crime. It put him in line for a violent death."

It shocked her out of her mood, as I hoped it would. She rose abruptly. "Don was involved in crime? You must be mistaken."

"There's no mistake. The Summer girl was in it too, if that's any satisfaction to you. You know about the high-jacking?"

"Yes. The sheriff was here tonight."

"What did the sheriff want?"

"I couldn't say. I wasn't in the room when they were talking. I could tell by the sound of the voices, though, that they were arguing. Apparently Don won."

"You didn't hear what they were arguing about?"

"No. When Brandon—when Sheriff Church was leaving, I asked him what the trouble was. He told me about the stolen truck."

"Did he seem suspicious of your husband?"

"No. He was very angry, but he didn't say a word about Don, one way or the other."

"When was he here?"

"About ten o'clock."

"Are you and the sheriff on a first-name basis?"

"Yes, I suppose we are, if it matters. Brandon's been

close to my family for years. My father and his father were close friends."

"I understood Church worked his way up from the bottom."

"His father was a barber, if that's what you mean. It didn't prevent my father from being his friend." When she spoke of her father, there was a change in her face, both hardening and refining. "Father was a democratic man, and a generous one. He helped to put Brandon through college."

"Could that have helped your husband to win his argument with Church?"

It took her a moment to catch my meaning. "Of course not. Brandon wouldn't be influenced by personal considerations."

"You're sure?"

"Perfectly sure. I know Brandon."

"And you're fond of him?"

"I wouldn't say I'm *fond* of him. I wonder if anyone is. I do admire him for what he's done. I respect his integrity."

"What has he done?"

"He came up from near the bottom, as you said. He's made himself the best sheriff we've ever had in this county. And I've known the others," she added. "Father was a Superior Court judge."

"Did your husband have anything to say about his brawl with Church?"

"It wasn't a brawl. They simply argued. No, Don wouldn't tell me anything. It's understandable, if he was involved in the crime as you say he was."

"He was."

"I don't understand how you can be so certain."

"I talked to the Summer girl tonight. She didn't know who I was, for a while anyway, and she said more than

she intended to. She and your husband and a man named
Bozey were all involved in the highjacking. You may have
seen this Bozey with your husband—a young hood with
red hair, eyes like a rabid dog. He wears a leather jacket
like a pilot's jacket."

"No, I never saw him." But the description seemed to
make the situation actual to her, perhaps for the first time.
"It can't be true! Don was at the court with me yesterday."

"All day?"

"Most of the afternoon. He came out after lunch to work
on the books. Then he started drinking in the office. He's
been drinking a great deal lately."

"Are you sure he didn't leave the office?"

"As sure as I can be. I didn't sit and watch him, naturally. But I'm absolutely certain he had nothing to do with
that shooting."

"He had plenty to do with it, Mrs. Kerrigan. Whether or
not he was there in person, he was one of those responsible."

"You mean that Don planned a cold-blooded murder,
for gain?"

"I'm pretty sure he planned the highjacking. The murder
was part of it. The two crimes can't be separated, so far
as I can see."

She said with a kind of awe: "I had no idea. I knew that
he was in trouble, I didn't realize how serious it was. He
should have told me," she whispered to herself. "He could
have had the house. Or anything."

I broke in on her self-recriminations: "There seems to be
more to this case than murder for gain. Your husband's
death throws the whole thing wide open."

"I thought you said that the girl—Jo Summer—"

"She's the logical suspect, of course. But I don't know.
They were set to go away together. She was in love with
him."

"In love with him?"

"In her way. In love with him and the easy life he promised her. They were going to Guatemala and live happily ever after."

"How can you know that?" Her face was a mask of pain.

"She told me herself. She wasn't lying. She may have been dreaming, but she wasn't lying. That wasn't the only interesting thing she said. It got a little involved, but the idea was that Anne Meyer had something to do with the highjacking. Tony Aquista told her a story about Anne Meyer which changed the original plan."

"What kind of a story?"

"I was hoping that you could tell me, Mrs. Kerrigan. I never got the story. The girl got suspicious and ran out on me."

Her eyes widened. Their dark blue depths were bottomless. She said slowly and carefully: "Why should you suppose that I would know anything about Anne Meyer?"

"You said quite a lot about her at the motor court, before we were interrupted. You wanted her found and shadowed, remember?"

"I'd prefer to forget it. I was almost crazy with jealousy. It's over now. Everything's over now. There's nothing left to be jealous of."

"Do you mean that something has happened to her?"

"I mean that my husband is dead. You can't be jealous of a dead man, can you? I was on the wrong track, anyway. She wasn't the one after all."

"She was at one time, you said."

"Yes, but it was finished. I was misled by something that happened last Friday. Don offered her the use of our place in the mountains for the weekend. She came here to pick up the keys, and I overheard the—transaction." Her voice took on a cutting edge: "He had no right to do it.

The cabin belongs to me. I guess that's what upset me."

"Where is the cabin?"

"On Lake Perdida. Father built it over twenty years ago, when they first put in the dam."

"Could the woman still be there?"

"I don't believe so. Don said not. When she failed to come to work on Monday, he drove up to the lake to see what was keeping her. But she was gone when he got there. At least, so he said."

"His story should be checked. Is there a telephone in the cabin?"

"No, there are no private telephones in the settlement. It's rather isolated."

"I'd like your permission to go up and make a search for her."

"Of course. If you think it will do any good."

"How do I get there?"

She gave me detailed instructions. The lake was on the western slope of the Sierra, about two hours of mountain driving from Las Cruces. "I'll get you the keys."

"Duplicates?"

"No, there's only the one set."

"Then she brought them back?"

"Don did, Monday night. Apparently she left them there."

"Was he gone all day Monday?"

"Yes, he was. He didn't come home until long past midnight."

"But he hadn't seen her?"

"He said he hadn't."

"Do you think he was telling the truth?"

"I have no idea," she said. "I lost track of Don years ago. No, I didn't ask him what he'd been doing all day."

"What do you think he was doing?"

"I have no idea."

She left the room and came back a minute later, with
two Yale keys and some smaller padlock keys clinking on
a chrome ring. "There you are. Good luck."

I said: "It might improve my luck if you don't mention
this to anyone. Especially anyone official."

"Brandon Church, you mean?"

"Yes."

"Have you been having trouble with him, too?"

"That's an understatement. Church hates my insides. He
seemed like a reasonable sort when I first met him, and
we were getting along. Then the whole thing went to
pieces. He's a friend of yours. What's on his mind?"

"I don't pretend to understand him. I know that he's a
good man. Father thought very highly of him." She managed a wan smile. "Could you be partly to blame for the
trouble between you?"

"I usually am, I guess."

"Perhaps he resents an outsider horning in. Brandon
takes his work very seriously. Don't worry, I won't say a
word to him about you." She offered me her hand. "I do
trust you, you see. I don't know exactly why I should—"

"Because you can. I wish you well. But I wouldn't go
around trusting people indiscriminately."

"You mean Brandon again, don't you?"

"I'm afraid so. A good man who goes sour—" I didn't
complete the sentence.

A high-powered engine was whining up the hill. It
stopped in front of the house. Kate Kerrigan went to the
window.

"Speak of the devil."

I looked out over her shoulder. Church climbed out of
his black Mercury and started up the concrete steps from
the street. Braga toiled along behind him like a fat Indian
wife. I went out the back door as they came in the front.

I drove east toward the phantom mountains. When I

was a few miles outside the city limits, something broke like a capsule behind my eyes. It leaked darkness through my brain and numbness through my body. I stopped the car on the shoulder of the road. Somewhere in the hills to the southwest, the Cyclops eye of the air beacon still scanned the starless sky. I wished that I was made of steel and powered by electricity.

I drove on slowly through the night-filled hills until I came to a tourist camp. I rented a cottage from a bleary-eyed boy and had a bad night's sleep, wrestling nightmare on a lumpy bed.

CHAPTER **15**: *Lake Perdida was a narrow body* of water held in place at six thousand feet by a concrete dam inserted in the slot between two timbered mountains. It was midmorning when I babied my hot engine over the top of the final grade and caught a glimpse of the lake between the trees. A cold wind from the Sierra peaks flawed its polished surface and soughed in the evergreens.

The blacktop followed the contours of the shore. I passed a tourist lodge, a roadside restaurant, a scattering of cottages. All of them were closed, and shuttered up for the winter. About midway in the lake's five- or six-mile length I came to a filling station which looked as if it might be open. I stopped in front of the gas pumps, which were sheltered under a portico made of unpeeled logs, and leaned on my horn.

When nothing happened, I got out and walked around my car. There was a handwritten announcement pinned to one of the uprights of the portico:

"Gone down the hill. Take water or air as needed, your welcome. For gas you'll have to wait. Back by ten (a.m.)"

I filled my steaming radiator and pushed on. Half a mile beyond the gas station a weathered wooden sign was attached to a pine tree on the upper side of the road: GREEN THOUGHT: CRAIG, LAS CRUCES. A smaller, newer metal sign: J. DONALD KERRIGAN, ESQ., was nailed below it. I turned up the rocky lane.

The cabin stood on a slope, hidden from the road by the trees. It was a large one-story house with a deep veranda. Its squared redwood timbers were gray with age. The shadow of the ancient trees hung over it like a foretaste of winter.

My feet rattled the boards of the veranda. The heavy wooden shutters that framed the windows were hanging open. I looked through the multipaned window beside the door into a dim deep room walled with oak paneling, roofed with slanting rafters. A Kodiak bearskin lay like something flattened by a steamroller in front of the stone fireplace at the far end.

I unlocked the door and went in. The air inside was chilly, and impregnated with the stale vestiges of a party. There were traces of a party in the main room. A brass ashtray on the redwood-bole coffee table was half full of cigarette ends, most of them smudged with lipstick. There were two dirty drinking glasses on the table, one marked with a telltale red crescent. Sniffing the glasses without touching them, I guessed that they had once contained good bourbon.

I went to the fireplace and felt the light wood ashes in the grate. The ashes were cold. As I stood up, I noticed something in the fur of the bearskin rug. It was a brown enameled woman's bobby pin. I searched the rug with my fingers and found another bobby pin. The bear's glass eyes were blasé. His teeth leered in a fixed lascivious grin.

I went through the sleeping-rooms. There was a big bunk-room with half a dozen two-tiered berths built along its walls. The layer of dust on the floor hadn't been disturbed for weeks or months. One of the two smaller bedrooms was equally disused. The other had been occupied more recently. The floor was swept. The maple bed had been slept in, and not made. I straightened out the tangled sheets. A limp rubber tube lay among them.

There were no clothes or luggage in the room, but there were several articles on top of the rustic bureau. A woman's nailfile, a jar of face cream standing open and beginning to dry out, a pair of tortoise-shell sun glasses, a number of bobby pins like the ones I had discovered in the bearskin. In the adjoining bathroom I found a tube of toothpaste and a toothbrush, lipstick, a bottle of estrogen oil. They accounted for the things that were missing from Anne Meyer's apartment in Las Cruces.

The kitchen was bright with chintz and knotty pine. A pot on the butane stove had remnants of spaghetti in the bottom, crawling with flies. The kitchen table had been set for two and not cleared, though the dishes were dirty. An empty wine bottle stood in the center of the table.

I left the kitchen to the languid autumn flies and let myself out the back door. Several cords of cut wood were piled under a tarpaulin against the rear wall. I looked under the tarpaulin and found black beetles. The outdoor brick oven in the yard was empty. A log outbuilding was cluttered with the remnants of past summers: canvas chairs, a small skiff, fishing tackle. I poked around in the outhouse and among the pine needles in the yard. Nothing.

I went back into the lodge through the kitchen door. There seemed to be a thickening and darkening of the air in the deserted rooms. In the living-room I had a moment of panic. I thought that one of the giant trees was going to crash down on the house. The irrational fear passed over quickly, but it left a sense of disaster. The glass-eyed bear in front of the dead fire, the blood-red cigarette ends in the dully gleaming ashtray, were infinitely dreary. I got out.

I locked the door behind me, not so much to keep intruders out as to keep the disaster in. It slipped through the walls and followed me down the lane, nagging at the nightmares in the back seat of my mind, where sex and death embraced.

The note had been removed from the front of the filling station. The door of the small stone building was standing open, and a gray-haired woman came out. She wore blue jeans and a battered man's felt hat with a trout fly stuck in the ribbon like a cockade.

"Hello there. You want gas?"

"It'll take about ten."

I handed her the keys and stood beside her while she manipulated the hose. Her face was square and weathered, and her eyes looked out of it like someone peering through a wall.

"You from L.A.?"

"I am."

"You're the first customer I've had today."

"It's getting pretty late in the season, isn't it?"

"Season's over, far as I'm concerned. I'm closing up this week and moving down the mountain before it snows. Old Mac at the Inn is the only human being that stays up here all winter. He can have it." Hanging up the dripping nozzle, she read the meter: "That will be three and a quarter."

I gave her a ten-dollar bill: I'd cashed a traveler's check at the place where I spent the night: and she made change from the pocket of her jeans.

"We get a lot of tourists from L.A. in the summer. What brings you up here so late?"

"Just looking around. I suppose you get plenty of people here from the valley towns?"

"Sure, they come up to get away from the heat. There's cottagers from all over—Fresno, Bakersfield, Las Cruces. I live in Fresno myself in the wintertime. My son's a junior at the college."

"Good for him."

"Ralph's a fine boy," she said, as if to rebut an argument to the contrary. "He appreciates me, even if some people don't. Ralph knows a good mother when he sees one. And he's not afraid of work, either. He helped me all summer with the station, and all fall he's been coming up weekends. Ralph's a real manly boy, not like some I could name."

"I like to hear of a boy like that." I was establishing myself with her, but I also happened to mean it. "I come across a lot of the other kind in my work."

"What sort of work is that?"

"I'm a detective."

"Oh. That must be interesting work. Ralph's father—Mr. Devore was a constable, before he took to—other things." She gave me a hard bright look over the pump. "Looking for somebody, mister?"

"You guessed it."

"There's nobody left up here, excepting me and old Mac and the foresters. The Inn is closed down for the winter." I followed her gaze through the trees and saw the brown peaked roofs of the Inn at the upper end of the lake. She turned back to me with something girlishly fearful in her eyes. "It isn't Ralph? He hasn't done anything wrong?"

"It's a young woman named Anne Meyer. I have a picture of her here."

She squinted at the snapshot of the laughing girl on the beach. "Yep," she said. "I thought so. I knew she wasn't up to any good."

"You've seen her?"

"Plenty of times. She used to come up here with that fourflusher that married Katie Craig."

"Kerrigan."

"That's the one. A fourflusher and a womanizer if I ever saw one." Her mouth was tight and grim. "Did Katie finally decide to divorce him?"

"You're a good guesser." Not good enough, but good.

"I'd say it's about time. I've known Katie Craig since she was knee-high. She was as bright and sweet a kid as you could ask for, only somehow she never learned to look out for herself. I don't mean to criticize the old Judge. He was a wonderful man, and it wasn't his fault. I guess it wasn't anybody's fault. She was engaged to marry Talley Raymond from San Francisco, then he got killed in the war and it knocked Katie for a loop, you might say. She married the wrong man, you can take my word for it. I know what it is to marry a wrong 'un myself." Her heavy neck flushed streakily. "When I think of the waste of a girl like that marrying a man like Kerrigan, it makes me heartsick. And then he had to come up here and turn the Judge's summer residence into a—a nest of concubines, that's what it is." The slow flush mounted her face under the tan. "I'm talking too much." She stared down intently at the snapshot in her hand, as if to focus her emotions on it.

"When did you see this woman last?"

"Monday, I guess it was. She spent the weekend up here, her first for a long time. I think it was the only time this summer. I was surprised to see her."

"Why?"

"Mr. Kerrigan has a new girl, that's why." She threw an intolerant glance in the general direction of the Inn. "Last summer it was different. This biddy used to drive up with him practically every weekend, bold as brass. I often used to wonder if Katie knew about it. I was tempted to write her a unanimous letter, but I never did."

"I'm interested in this last weekend," I said.

"Well, she came in here on Saturday afternoon, asked me for water. Her radiator was boiling. Mine boiled, too, when I saw her. I had half a mind to tell her that there was plenty of water in the lake and she could take a running jump in it. But Ralph wouldn't have liked that. He was here, and he tells me I got to maintain good public relations. That's the way Ralph talks."

"What kind of a car was she driving?"

"Black Chrysler convertible. Lord knows where she got the money to pay for it. The Devil knows, anyways."

"Was she alone?"

"For a change she was. But she was all prissied up and dressed to kill, and I said to myself at the time: 'You're meeting a man and you don't have to try the innocent act on me.' She was, too."

"Did Kerrigan show up later?"

"She didn't come up to spend the weekend knitting. I saw them together Monday. For all I know he was in the cabin with her the whole weekend. I had better things to do over the weekend than spy on him and his hussy. But Monday afternoon I was coming back from fishing and I passed them on the road. They were headed toward the Inn."

"Both of them? Kerrigan and Anne Meyer?"

"If that's her name. Leastwise, he had a woman with him. I didn't see her face—she had a hat on—but it must of been her."

"Would you swear to it?"

She looked a little flustered for a moment. "Sure I would, if Katie needs it for her divorce."

"Are you sure it wasn't Mrs. Kerrigan herself?"

"Naw. I'd know Katie if she had a potato sack over her

head. It wasn't her. It was this one." She flourished the picture.

I took it out of her hand. "Was she driving?"

"No, he was. She was leaning back in the seat with her face sort of turned into the corner. Which is why I didn't get a decent look at her. Not that I was missing much."

I said: "Mrs. Devore—do I have your name right?"

"Yep."

"This woman you saw in the car with Kerrigan. Are you sure she was alive?"

Her face went ugly with surprise. She looked like a bewildered bulldog. "That's some question, mister."

"Can you answer it?"

"Not for sure I can't. I didn't see her move or talk, but she certainly didn't *look* dead. Is she supposed to be dead?"

"This is Friday. She was last seen Monday, unless you've seen her since."

"Nope, I haven't seen her. What goes on, anyway?"

"Murder. There's quite an epidemic of it running in Las Cruces."

"Holy cow." Her jaw pushed forward and the lower teeth scraped at the few black hairs on her upper lip. "Maybe Ralph was right at that."

"Right about what?"

"About this fellow that came here Saturday night. He knocked on the door about ten o'clock, wanted the use of a phone. I told him we didn't have one—the only phone up here belongs to the forest service. The little whipper-snapper didn't believe me. He got mad and wanted to make a personal issue out of it: something about how he was a Mex and that was why I wouldn't let him in. I told him, shucks, said I got no feeling against Mexicans. He didn't believe that either."

"What did he look like?"

"Well, he looked like a Mex to me, though he didn't

talk like one. He talked pretty good English, just as good
as me. But he was dark-complected and he had that dead
black hair, sort of curly. And those big black eyes they
have. I never seen such eyes in a man's head. They rolled
around in their sockets like he was off his rocker. That's
what Ralph thought, too. Lucky Ralph was here. He
practically had to throw him out on his ear."

"Did you say he was a small man?"

"Compared to you or Ralph he was. Medium-sized.
Pretty well built at that, but I almost had to laugh when
he wanted to fight with Ralph."

"What did he say?"

"Something about he had an important telephone call
and could he use our phone. I said, sure, if we had one,
only we don't. Then he got sassy, started to call me names.
That's when Ralph stepped in. Ralph grabbed him by the
collar of his jacket and marched him out to his car. He
was screaming at Ralph in Spanish. Ralph said after, it
was just as well I don't know any Spanish.

"Ralph didn't think it was very funny, though. *He* could
handle the fellow all right, but he was worried about other
people. He said in his opinion the fellow was dangerous.
Borderline psychopath, I think he said, something like
that. Ralph is a real deep student of psychology. He said
you can often tell them by their eyes: they get that vacant
look in their eyes like there was nobody home. This one
certainly had it. So maybe he's the one you're looking for?"
Her face was transfigured, bright with curiosity.

"I found him yesterday, if it was the man I think it
was."

"And he committed a murder?"

"He was involved in one."

"Who is he?"

"His name is Tony Aquista," I said. "Getting back to

Monday afternoon, you said that Kerrigan was driving the woman's car toward the Inn?"

"Yessir."

"What about the old man at the Inn?"

"MacGowan, you mean? He's the caretaker."

"Did he see them after you did?"

"I wouldn't know. I haven't been talking to him this last month." Her mouth clamped tight on itself again. "Not since the old rounder let his granddaughter take up with Kerrigan. He's irresponsible, an old fool, that's what he is."

"Is she the new girl you mentioned? Kerrigan's girl?"

"She went off to Las Cruces with him last month and hasn't been back. What do you think?"

"I think her name's Jo Summer. Am I right?"

"Josephine. Josephine MacGowan. He calls her Jo all right, but you got your signals mixed on her last name."

"Somebody has. Is MacGowan over there now?"

"Unless he changed his habits. He never goes anywhere. I don't think he drives down the hill more than once a year."

I thanked her for her information and started to climb into my car.

"Listen, mister, what's been going on in Las Cruces? Is Katie Craig all right?"

"She was a few hours ago. But her husband isn't. He's dead."

"Is he the one that got murdered?"

"One of them."

"Katie didn't have anything to do with it, did she?"

"No," I said. "She didn't."

"Thank goodness for that. I've always had a soft spot in my heart for Katie, though I haven't seen her now for a couple of years. Taught her to tie flies when she was just a little yellow-haired tomboy." Her eyes were luminous with old memories. "It's terrible to see the years pass, and the suffering they bring to people. I know how Katie has suffered."

So did I.

CHAPTER 16: *The Inn was a rambling two-story* building faced with weathered brown shingles. Its shuttered windows seemed to doze in the sun. The mountainside rose behind it, and farther back, in the eastern distance, the high Sierras thrust their bald white domes toward the stratosphere.

I parked in front of the rustic log veranda and walked up a gravel road that led around to the back. A gray squirrel scampered away from the crunch of my footsteps, looking back a couple of times to make sure he was being noticed. A bluejay jeered at me from the limb of a spruce. I told him to keep a civil tongue in his head.

A gray-bearded man in overalls appeared on the other side of the spruce. He walked with an awkward hitch and roll. Resting one hand against the trunk of the tree, he squinted up at the bird with a gap-toothed grin. "Don't pay any attention to him. He thinks he owns the place."

The jay jumped up and down in a small blue fury. He swooped at the man's gray head, firing staccato bursts of sound. The old man waved him away, laughing in a voice almost as high and feckless as the bird's. The bird flew up into the top of the tree and swung there like a bright blue Christmas-tree ornament.

"He's the king of the castle," the old man said, or chanted, "and we're the dirty rascals." His eyes were black and bright under unkempt gray eyebrows.

"Mr. MacGowan?"

He stroked his neck with the side of his hand. "That's my name. You have the advantage of me."

"Archer. Lew Archer. I'm a private detective working with the police on a disappearance."

"Disappearance?" He pronounced the word with a faint Scots accent, imported long ago.

"A woman has turned up missing in Las Cruces."

"What woman is it? Not Josephine?"

"Who's she?"

A look of suspicion that went with his accent puckered the skin around his eyes. "I can't say for certain that that's any of your business, mister."

"Forget it."

"All right."

I let the question of Josephine ride for the present. "The missing woman's name is Anne Meyer. She was seen up here last weekend, by Mrs. Devore at the filling station. Mrs. Devore thought you might be able to help me."

"Mrs. Devore thinks a lot of things. Not half as many things as she says, though. What's it got to do with me?"

"She saw the woman driving with Kerrigan on Monday afternoon. They were headed in this direction. Do you know Donald Kerrigan?"

"I ought to," he said darkly. "Yeah, I saw them Monday. They went past here up the road to the corrals."

"Can you describe the woman?"

He wagged his white head. "I never did get close enough to make out her physog. I think she was a young woman. She had on a dark brown suit, and some kind of a funny hat on her head. I believe her hair was dark."

"You saw all this as the car went by?"

"Nope. I didn't say that. You're putting words into my mouth." He leaned his bowed shoulders against the tree-trunk and looked up into the branches. His scraggly beard pointed at me accusingly.

"Sorry. I misunderstood you."

"All right, then. I saw this Kerrigan drive past, and I

didn't know but what the woman with him—" He broke
off, coughing behind his hand. "I mean to say, it so happens I've a bone to pick with Kerrigan. A private matter.
I thought: here's my chance to have a word with him. He
couldn't go far in that direction: the road ends up above
the stables. So I followed along on foot. It took me quite
a while to get up there. I don't walk so good since I broke
my hip. Time was when I could run up a little hill like
that and not even change my breathing. I was a great
rock-climber when I was a lad back across the water."

There were continental distances in his eyes, and his
old mind was spiraling off across them. I showed him
Anne Meyer's picture to bring him back to the point.

"Was this the woman with Kerrigan?"

"Maybe it was," he answered slowly. "Then again maybe it wasn't. I told you I never did get close up to her.
When I reached the top of the hill behind the stables, I
saw them through the trees. They were down in the hollow
below the water tank, digging a hole."

"Doing what?"

"There's no call to shout, my hearing is perfectly good.
They were digging a hole."

"What kind of a hole?"

"Just a common ordinary hole in the ground. It went
through my mind that maybe they shot a deer illegally
and they were burying it. I yelled at them to stop, that it
was private property they were on. I guess I ought to've
waited and crept up on them. But these last few years by
myself, I get mad awful easy."

"Especially at Kerrigan?"

"You know him, eh? You should have seen him jump
when I let out that yell. He ran for the car, with the
woman at his heels. It was parked on the other side of
the water tank where the road loops round, so I had no

chance to catch them. I got a good shovel out of it, though."
A mischievous smile creased his face, and he looked like a
withered boy in a false beard. "You want to see it?"

"I'd rather see the hole. Can we drive up there?"

"I guess so. Only, I warn you it isn't much to look at.
It's just a hole. Course if you've never seen a hole—" He
emitted a high jaybird chuckle.

"Hell," I said, "I'm in one."

A few hundred yards past the Inn, the road meandered
up the hillside, dwindling to a rutted dirt track. We passed
a sunlit clearing occupied by stables and corrals. Behind
them the hill rose steeply, its rise accentuated by tall trees
that grew up along it in desultory ranks. I caught sight
of a wooden water tank standing high on scaffolding at
the top. We crawled up the hairpinning lane toward it in
low gear.

I stopped the car in a green tunnel made by overarch-
ing trees.

"Down there," MacGowan said.

He led me across a granite ridge projecting like a broken
rib from the earth, and down into the hollow. The hole
was about six feet long by two feet wide. It was roughly
the shape of a grave, but shallower, no more than a foot
deep. A pile of sandy earth mixed with pine needles stood
beside it. I got down on my knees and tested the bottom
of the hole with my fingers. The earth at the bottom was
still impacted. It hadn't been dug deeper and filled in.

"I gave you fair warning it wasn't much to look at," the
old man said behind me. "Wonder what those darn fools
thought they were doing. Digging for buried treasure?"

I stood up and turned to MacGowan. "Who was doing
the digging?"

"She was."

"Was he holding a gun on her, anything like that?"

"Not that I saw. Maybe he had one in his pocket. He was standing right here where I am, with his hands in his pockets. It's just the sort of thing he would do, letting a woman do his dirty work."

"When they ran away, did you say he went first?"

"That's correct. I bet he hasn't run that fast in years. She had a hard time keeping up. Matter of fact, she took a tumble before she got up to the road."

"Where did she fall?"

"I'll show you."

We climbed the far side of the hollow, where the lane looped around and swung back downhill. He pointed into the shallow ditch beside it. It was overgrown with manzanita bushes whose branches were red and shiny as if they had been freshly dipped in blood.

"Right about here," he said. "He was in the car already when she fell. He didn't get out and help her, either, fat slob that he is."

"You're not very fond of Kerrigan, are you?"

"No sir, I'm not. I've no cause to be."

"What was the bone you had to pick with him?"

"I don't much like to talk about it. It's a family affair, having to do with my granddaughter. She's only a young girl—"

He saw that I wasn't listening, and broke off. My eye had caught a glint of something among the manzanitas. It was the heel of a woman's shoe, wedged in the crack between two granite boulders. Several bright bent nails protruded from the top. I pried it loose with my fingers: a heel of medium height, tipped with rubber and covered with scuffed brown leather.

"Looks as if she lost a heel," he said. "I noticed she walked peculiar when she got up. Thought maybe she hurt her leg."

"Where did they go from here?"

"There's only the one way *to* go." He pointed downhill.

From where we stood, I could see the mercury trickle of the lake between the trees. The sun hung over it like a great silent blowtorch. Below the white lip of the dam, the powerhouse and its company town were hidden. The purple walls of the canyon beyond sloped down and away, dissolving in hot white distance. Under the white valley haze Las Cruces lay out of sight. It was hard to imagine from the cool forest height, but I knew that it was there, with fifty thousand people sweltering in its streets. I looked down at the leather object in my hand, and wondered which of the fifty thousand was Cinderella.

CHAPTER **17**: *I took MacGowan home. He*

lived in a small brown cottage behind the Inn. It had a peaked roof like a Swiss chalet, and fading yellow sunflowers painted on the front door. To my surprise, he invited me in for a cup of tea.

He pronounced it "tay," as if he liked the Old World flavor of the word. There was something Old World, too, about his living-room, which was crowded with ancient tobacco-colored furniture. Some outdated copies of *Punch* lay on the table beside the battery radio. There were pictures on the wall from the *Illustrated London News,* and a few old photographs.

One was an enlarged snapshot of a muscular man in shirt-sleeves who had his arm around a sunbonneted woman. They were standing in front of a white frame house, smiling at each other. Though the house was ugly and boxlike, the people poorly dressed, there was something idyllic about the scene. The smiles had a prewar innocence. I looked more closely at them and saw that the man was MacGowan, beardless and in his prime.

The old man limped out of the kitchen. "Kettle will soon be boiling. Have a seat."

"You're very kind."

"The shoe's on the other foot. I welcome a visitor. I haven't had one for a month, and it's lonely living since my old woman died." He indicated the enlargement with his thumb. "That's her and I, taken twenty-five years ago. I wasn't always a kind of a hermit like I am now."

"You stay up here all winter by yourself?"

"I do."

"I couldn't stand the loneliness."

He sat down stiffly in an old plush armchair, which emitted a puff of dust under his weight. Some of the dust was caught in the light from the window, and swirled there like boiling gold.

"There's different kinds of loneliness, mister—what did you say your name was?"

"Lew Archer."

"Different kinds of loneliness," he repeated. "The kind you make for yourself is the best. You get a certain satisfaction out of living alone, not needing anybody else, especially when you're old. You know, a man gets weary batting around in the world. I've done a lot of things in my time, sailed A.B. from Glasgow, raised wheat in Manitoba, mined silver in Nevada and copper in the Traverse mines. I was a janitor in San Berdoo before I came up here. But the city never suited me just right. I used to go back to Traverse just about every year for my vacation."

"I don't think I've heard of Traverse. Is it in California?"

"Yeah, over near the Nevada border." He pointed at the enlarged snapshot again. "That picture was taken in Traverse in the old days, when there were more than a thousand souls in the place. It's just a ghost town now, nothing left but the buildings, and most of them are sliding downhill.

The mine's worked out, you see. Last time I was there, three-four years ago, there wasn't a single living human being." He smiled reminiscently. "It suited me fine after San Berdoo."

"Did you have any other family besides your wife?" I wanted to get back to the subject of his granddaughter.

"I had a son," he said. "He'd be about your age now. He was killed in an accident at Terminal Island. They gave him a draft exemption because he worked in the shipyards, and then they went ahead and killed him anyway. I didn't see much of him for a long time before that, though. He took up with a Filipino girl, and I didn't think too well of the idea."

His mind veered in the light and shifting wind of his own feelings: "It wasn't Jo's fault she grew up a little wild. Her mother married again—another Filipino this time—and they let the lass run those Long Beach streets when she should of been in school."

"You're talking about your granddaughter?"

"Yes. She's living in Las Cruces now. You don't happen to know her?"

"I may at that," I said casually. "What's her name?"

"I disremember her married name, but she calls herself Jo Summer most of the time. It's kind of a stage name, she wants to be a professional singer. Maybe you've heard her sing at that nightclub in Las Cruces—the Golden Slipper?"

"No, but I've met her."

He leaned forward in the creaking armchair. "What do you think of the place she's working in? It's a pretty low-down dive, isn't it?"

"I'm afraid it is."

"That's what I told her," he said. "I told her no young married woman should take a job in a public bar like that. Not with a boss like Kerrigan anyway. But she wouldn't listen. I'm too old and she's too young, and we can't talk to each other. She thinks I'm an old fool. Maybe I am, but I can't help worrying about her. Was she all right when you saw her?"

I didn't have to answer. The kettle chirred and began to whistle. MacGowan went into the kitchen. While he made the tea, I tried to figure out what to say to him.

He brewed it black and bitter, like my thoughts.

"This is good tea," was what I finally said.

He blinked in acknowledgment over his tilted cup. It was a decent piece of china, decorated with an old-fashioned pink-and-gold flower pattern. He set it down gently on the table beside him.

"You ought to hear her sing. Not that jazzy stuff she sings in the nightclub, but some of the old songs, *Annie Laurie, Comin' through the Rye*. I got her to sing them for me when she was visiting here."

"When was that?"

"Last month. She came up the hill around the first of September, brought her husband with her." His black eyes fastened on my face. "Do you know her husband, too? I don't recall his name."

"What does he look like?"

"I didn't like the looks of him, to tell the truth. He's a redheaded lad—"

"Bozey?"

"That's the name. You know him, eh?"

"Not very well."

"What sort of a boy is he?" His face had darkened, sinking on its bones. "I'll tell you why I ask. He didn't act the way a young husband should act on his honeymoon."

"It was their honeymoon?"

"So they said. I had my doubts about it. It's a nasty thought, but I even doubted they were properly married. He didn't treat her with proper respect. Are they getting along?"

"I wouldn't know. I do know he's a rough customer. See the marks on my face?"

"I'd have to be blind not to see them. I didn't like to mention them."

"Bozey gave them to me."

"He did? With his iron knucks?"

"Don't tell me he worked you over."

"He never got a chance to," MacGowan said grimly. "I kicked him out bag and baggage before he could try anything on me. But it was touch-and-go there for a minute."

"What happened?"

"I was doing my washing that day, the day he left. They were some place outside and I opened up their suitcase to see if they had anything needed washing. Shook out one of his dirty shirts, and it had a gun wrapped in it, an automatic pistol, and a pair of iron knucks. That didn't look too good to me. I rummaged around some more and found the money in the bottom of the suitcase."

"Money?"

"Yep. A lot of money, wrapped in old newspapers. Big bills, too. There must of been thousands of dollars. It didn't make sense to me—an able-bodied bum like him who couldn't even afford a hotel honeymoon. So when they came back, I asked him about the money. And the knucks. And the gun."

"That was a brave thing to do."

"Don't worry, I took precautions. I loaded my deer-rifle and held it across my knees while I was talking to him. He looked like he wanted to kill me, but the rifle held him off."

"What did he say?"

"He didn't say very much of anything. Just called me a few bad names and walked into the bedroom and got his suitcase and put it in his car and drove away. Jo didn't want him to go, but he paid no attention to what she said. He dropped her like a hotcake. I guess you can hardly blame her for taking up with Kerrigan after that." A puzzled frown wrinkled his forehead. "But now you tell me she's back with Bozey again?"

"More or less."

"Is he a robber or something like that?"

"Something like that. Did he ever talk to you about his background?"

"Not very much. He was only here a couple of days. Let me think. He mentioned New Mexico once or twice, did a little bragging about his connections in Albuquerque."

"What kind of connections?"

"Business connections. I think he said something about the liquor business. But I knew he was a fourflusher, and I didn't pay much attention."

"You must have asked Jo about him after he left."

"Yeah, but she didn't know much. She said she only met him the week before, in Los Angeles. I tried to talk her out of going back to him." He stirred uneasily. "I guess I better go and see her again."

"You might have a long way to go."

He looked at me questioningly.

"Mr. MacGowan, how is your health? Is your heart in good shape?"

He was flattered by my interest, and thumped himself on the chest. "Nothing the matter there. Why?"

"Your granddaughter's in trouble."

"Jo in trouble? Is it serious?"

"Yes. She's wanted for car theft and on suspicion of murder. Kerrigan was shot last night. I saw her running away from the place where it happened."

He was silent for a long time. The minutes droned like dying flies in the corners of the room. His body seemed to shrink in the chair.

"You've been making a fool of me," he said at last. "Why didn't you tell me?"

"I didn't want to hurt you."

"Hurt me?" His bearded mouth was twisted. "I knew Jo was headed for trouble. I did what I could to stop her. I went down to Las Cruces and tried to shake her loose from Kerrigan, from Kerrigan and that town of his. When you've seen as much of the world as I have—" His hand swept sideways in a brusque blind movement that sent his teacup crashing to the floor.

I got down on my knees and started to pick up the pieces. I felt that it was the least I could do, and the most.

Leaning above me, he said thinly: "Did she murder him?"

"I don't know."

"You said she stole a car. Why did she have to do that? I would have given her money, all I've got."

"It was transportation she needed, and she needed it then. Maybe she intended to come up here to you."

I looked up at him. He wagged his head slowly from side to side. "She didn't come to me."

I finished gathering the thin white pieces in the unbroken saucer, and set it on the table. He picked up one translucent shard and held it to the light.

"That was the last of the set. We bought it the year we were married, in the Hudson's Bay Company store in Winnipeg. Augh." He dropped it back into the saucer. "No use crying over spilt milk. Thanks for your trouble, boy."

There was another silence.

"What happened to her husband, if that's what he is?"

"Bozey's wanted, too, and on the run. He highjacked a truckload of whisky. The driver was killed."

"Another one killed?"

"That's right. Do you have any idea where Bozey could have run to? Or Jo?"

"I should say not." He levered himself out of the chair and stood looking down at me. "What about this woman that's missing, the one that lost her heel? Where does she come into all this?"

"That's the question I have to answer. One of them." I got up and moved to the door. "I'm driving back to Las Cruces now. Can I give you a lift?"

"Thank you kindly, I'll drive myself. I need a chance to think. I need a little time to take this in."

"If Jo turns up here, will you let me know? You can reach me through Mrs. Kerrigan."

"I don't know about that," he said. "Maybe I will and maybe I won't. Augh, she won't come here anyway, not to me."

He opened the door for me. The fierce sun clawed at his face.

CHAPTER **18**:   *I drove back through the green* silence along the lake-shore road. Passing the Kerrigan cabin, I saw the red convertible parked in the entrance to the lane. Mrs. Kerrigan waved at me frantically through the windshield. I left my car at the roadside and went to hers.

She was beautifully dressed and groomed, in black silk and a black hat and black gloves. Except for her eyes and mouth, her face was colorless.

"I didn't expect to see you," I said.

"Sally Devore told me where you were. I knew you had to come back this way. I've been waiting."

"For these?"

I brought her keyring out of my pocket and handed it in through the window. It jangled nervously in her gloved hand.

"It isn't why I came," she said. "Now that I'm here, though, I'd like to see the cabin. Will you come up with me?"

"I wouldn't go in if I were you."

"Is she there? I knocked on the door and no one answered. Is she hiding inside?"

"No. She's nowhere around. Anne Meyer's dropped out of sight, as your husband said."

"But he was lying to me about Monday. Mrs. Devore saw them together on Monday."

"Apparently she did. So did old MacGowan at the Inn. He caught them in the woods, doing a rather peculiar thing."

A faint flush appeared on her cheekbones. "Were they making love?"

"Hardly. She was digging a hole in the ground. Your husband was watching her dig."

"A hole? I don't understand."

"Neither do I. Do you mind if I get in?"

"Of course. Please do."

She slid over in the seat, making room for me behind the wheel. I showed her the brown leather heel.

"Do you recognize this?"

She took it from me and held it up to the light. "I believe I do. Who is it supposed to belong to?"

"You tell me."

"Anne Meyer?"

"Are you guessing, or do you know?"

"I can't be absolutely certain. I think she was wearing shoes like this when I saw her last Friday. Where did you get this?"

"In the woods. She seems to have lost it when Mac-Gowan frightened them off."

"I see." She dropped the heel in my hand as if it was tainted. "Why in the world were they digging a hole in the woods?"

"Not they. She was digging. He was standing there watching her. It raises a lot of questions, and one possible answer. I've heard of sadistic murderers taking their victims to a lonely place and forcing them to dig their own graves. If he was planning to kill her—"

"But it's incredible." The words exploded softly from her mouth. "Don couldn't have done a thing like that."

"You told me he was a sadist."

"I didn't mean it that way. I was speaking loosely." She was gripping the door-handle as if we were going around a curve at high speed.

"So am I. It's merely a possibility that occurred to me." I offered her a cigarette, which she refused, and lit one for myself. "Did you see him Monday night when he came home?"

"Yes. It was very late, but I was still awake."

"Did he say anything to you at all?"

"I don't remember. No. I was in bed. He didn't come to bed. He sat up drinking. I heard him prowling around the house for a long time. Eventually I took a sleeping-pill." Her hand shifted from the door-handle to my arm. "How can you say he killed her? You don't even know that she's dead."

"No, but the signs are bad. If she isn't dead, where is she?"

"Are you asking me?" The pressure of her hand was almost painful. Her eyes were a tragic blue black. "You can't believe that I killed her?"

"That's true. I can't."

She didn't seem to notice my denial. "I was at home all day Monday. I can prove it. I had a friend with me all afternoon. She came for lunch and stayed until nearly dinnertime. Do you know who she was?"

"It doesn't matter. You don't have to prove an alibi for me."

"I can, though, and I want to. It was Marion Westmore who was with me—the District Attorney's wife. We were planning the Junior League rummage sale. It seems such an awfully long time ago, more like four years than four days. And what a silly way to spend an afternoon."

"You think so?"

"I do now. Everything seems silly to me now. Did you ever have the feeling that time had stopped for you? That you were living in a vacuum, without a future or even a past?"

"I had it once," I said. "The week after my wife left me. But it didn't last. It won't last for you, either. You'll get over it."

"I didn't know you had a wife."

"That was a long time ago."

"Why did she leave you?"

"She said she couldn't stand the life I led. That I gave too much to other people and not enough to her. And I guess she was right in a way. But it really boiled down to the fact that we weren't in love any more. At least, one of us wasn't."

"Which one?"

"I'd rather not go into it. Exhuming corpses is an ugly business."

The rebuff held her silent for a time. She looked out toward the lake, which glimmered like fragments of fallen sky between the trees.

"I suppose I asked for that," she said. "You have been kind to me, though, last night, and again today. I can't help wondering if it's simply a technique. Is this your crimeside manner, Mr. Archer? Your psychological third-degree?"

There was enough truth in the question to make me wince. "I'm playing it as straight as I can with you. I don't deny I've been tempted to use people, play on their feelings, push them around. Those are the occupational diseases of my job."

"And you don't have them?"

"I have them." Jo Summer's changing smile wavered smokily behind my eyes. "This is a dirty business I'm in. All I can do is watch myself and keep it as clean as I can."

I felt as if she'd put me on the spot, and I changed the direction of the conversation: "What brought you up here, anyway?"

"I don't know for certain. Perhaps I simply wanted to see you again." She wouldn't look at me. "Is that a dreadful confession for a woman to make to a man?"

"Dreadful. You shock me, Katie."

"No, don't make fun of me. There's nothing funny about it. Brandon Church frightened me when I talked to him last night—this morning."

"Did he make things unpleasant for you?"

"Not exactly. He didn't accuse me of anything. But he seemed so different—not the man I knew at all. He hardly seemed to know me, he treated me like a stranger. I wondered if he was drugged, or losing his mind. And then the other one, the Spanish American deputy—"

"Braga?"

"Yes. Sal Braga. I heard him threaten your life. He said he would shoot you on sight, and Brandon didn't even try to quiet him. Brandon didn't say a word."

"He probably likes the project."

"But why? What's happening to all of us?"

"That's my problem. There are a few more questions I'd like to ask you."

"About Brandon? He was one person I thought I knew. I don't seem to know anyone, really."

"About your husband and Anne Meyer, if you can stand talking about them."

She answered after a pause, in a neutral tone: "I don't mind."

"All right. Were they still attached to each other?"

"I don't believe so. He told me that he broke with her months ago. For once I think he was telling the truth. When I saw them together at the motor court, they didn't act as if—" Her voice faded.

"As if they were still lovers?"

She nodded.

"Have you any idea why they broke off, assuming that they did?"

"I suppose he got tired of her—he tired of women very easily. Or she got bored with him." There was a glint of malice in her eyes. "She was just as promiscuous as he was."

"But they were still friendly after the break?"

"Apparently they were. She went on working for him, until last week."

"You say she was promiscuous. How much do you know about her?"

"I know a good deal about Anne. So much that I can even feel sorry for her, when I'm not feeling sorry for myself. You see, I've known her ever since we were in high school together. I'm only two or three years older than she is. Anne had a bad reputation even then."

"In high school?"

"Yes, she started young. She was one of the boy-crazy ones, very pretty and very wild. It wasn't entirely her own fault. She grew up terribly fast. She was a full-grown woman before she was fifteen. And she had no decent home life. Her mother was dead, and her father was a bestial man. Really bestial."

"You sound as if you made a study of them."

"Father did," she said surprisingly. "He was deeply concerned about Anne and her family, and he discussed it with me. He was judge of the Juvenile Court as well as Superior Court, and he had the disposition of the case. He had to decide what was to be done with Anne after it happened."

"What did happen?"

She wouldn't meet my eyes. "Her father assaulted her."

"Do you mean what I think you mean?"

"Yes."

"Why isn't Meyer in San Quentin?"

"She wouldn't testify against him in court. Of course she was the only witness, so they had no case. But they did have enough to take her away from him, out of his house. Father intended to put her in a foster home, but it turned out not to be necessary. Brandon married her sister—he was Juvenile Officer in those days—and the two of them took her in. She lived with them for several years, and it seems to have worked out. There was no more trouble with Anne, no more legal trouble anyway."

"Until now."

She twisted suddenly in the seat and looked up the lane toward the hidden cabin. Her half-turned body made a breathtaking line against the light.

"Won't you come up to the cabin with me?"

"What for?"

"I want to see what sort of condition it's in. I intend to sell it."

"You better stay out of there."

"Why? Is her body—?"

"Nothing like that. You simply wouldn't like it in there. In fact you'd better give me back the keys."

"I don't understand why." But she took the keyring out of her black suède bag and handed it to me. "What do you want them for?"

"I'll turn them over to the authorities if I can find an honest cop in Las Cruces. You should know some honest cops, if your father was a judge."

"I thought Brandon was one. I still believe he is, when he's himself." She bit her lip. "Why don't you go to Sam Westmore?"

"The District Attorney?"

"Yes. Sam and Marion are my oldest friends. You can rely on Sam Westmore." But she was holding onto the door-handle again, as if she needed it to anchor her to reality. "Is it safe, though, for you to go back to the city?"

"I don't know if it's safe. It should be interesting."

She said in a small, clear voice: "You're a brave man, aren't you?"

"Not brave. Merely stubborn. I don't like to see the jerks and hustlers get away with too much. Or they might take over entirely."

"You won't let them, will you?"

Her voice was dreamy, almost childish. Her gentian eyes were wide and dewy. They closed. I took her head between my hands and kissed her mouth.

Her hat fell off, but she didn't try to retrieve it. Her head rested on my shoulder like a ruffled golden bird. Her breast leaned on me, and I could feel the quickened movement of her breathing.

"You'll stop them," she said.

"If they don't stop me first, Katie."

"How did you know my name was Katie? Nobody's called me Katie for a long time."

I didn't answer. An explanation would only spoil the moment.

It ended anyway. She stiffened and drew back. When I tried to reach her mouth again, she turned her head away.

"God," she said harshly. "I need a keeper, don't I? I warned you not to be sympathetic to me. I'm ready to weep on any shoulder that offers itself."

The red convertible followed me down the mountain. I kept remembering the taste of her mouth.

CHAPTER **19**:   *I found Meyer in a cubicle in the* corner of his warehouse, sitting idle at an invoice-strewn desk. He looked at my face as if the sight of it hurt his red-rimmed eyeballs.

"What happened to you?"

"I cut myself shaving."

"What were you using, a power mower? I was commencing to think you ran out on me. Which maybe you should of at that. Brand wants me to take you off the case."

"So?"

"So nothing. I don't take orders from any young snot-nose that I helped to put in the courthouse with my good money." Meyer leaned forward on his arms, his face like the graying mask of an old fox. "Only I wouldn't do anything more to cross him if I was you. Brand is a bad one to cross."

"I don't take it so well myself."

"Maybe not." He squinted ironically at my damaged face. "But you're not sheriff. Now where you been?"

"Lake Perdida."

"Why go traipsing off there? I been trying to contact you all day, and I'm not the only one. The D.A. wants to see you. While you've been pooping off around the countryside, this case has been breaking open. You know the Buick that got left at the airbase—"

"I ought to. I was the one who reported it."

"Anyway, they traced it to a car-dealer in Los Angeles. This redhead—what's his name?"

"Bozey."

"This Bozey bought it off a used-car lot around the first of September. He paid cash for it, a five-hundred-dollar bill and some smaller bills. When the dealer tried to deposit the money in his bank, the cashier caught it."

"Hot?"

"It scorched his fingers. The money was part of the loot from a bank in Portland that got robbed last August. The bank in L.A. had a circular from the Oregon police listing the numbers of the bills. It was a big haul, over twenty thousand bucks altogether."

"Bozey took a bank for twenty grand?"

Meyer nodded his shaggy head. "There's a two-thousand-dollar reward out for the redhead. That should keep you on the ball. If anything will. What sent you up to the lake, for God's sake? Maybe you thought you'd get in a little fishing on my time?"

I almost walked out on him. One thing kept me: I needed more time with Meyer.

"Call it fishing. I caught something." I laid the scuffed brown heel on the desk. "Does this belong to your daughter Anne?"

He turned it over in his fingers, gently, as if it possessed a feminine sensitivity. "I wouldn't know if it's Annie's or not. I never paid much attention to what a woman wears. Where did it come from?"

I told him.

"That don't sound so good for Annie." He rolled the heel on the desk like a misshapen dice. "What do you make of it?"

I leaned on a bookkeeper's stool against the wall and lit a cigarette. "I have a hunch that she was digging a grave. It could have been intended for her, or somebody else."

"Who else? Kerrigan?"

"Not Kerrigan. He was superintending the job."

"It don't make sense to me. Are you sure it was Annie with him?"

"I have a couple of witnesses. Neither of them made a positive identification, but I think they're just being cautious. If this heel is hers, it clinches it."

He picked it up from the litter on the desk, and scratched his stubbly chin with the exposed nails. The sound rasped on my nerve-ends.

"Hilda would know, maybe."

He reached for the telephone and dialed a number. On the plywood wall behind his head the end of an old motto protruded from under a bright new girlie calendar:

> *I married a woman*
> *But that came to an end.*
> *Get a good dog, boys,*
> *He will be your friend.*

Meyer spoke into the mouthpiece: "Hello, Brand, is Hilda around?"

The telephone squawked negatively.

"Know where she is?"

The sheriff's voice was denatured by its passage through the wires, but recognizable: "No. I don't." His voice sank, and I missed the rest of what he said.

Meyer listened with a lengthening face. "Well, what do you know about that? Personally I think she's making a big mistake, and I'll tell her that if I see her." He dropped the receiver. "Brand says she's gone and left him. Packed her clothes and moved out."

"Did he say why?"

"Not him. But I happen to know they never did get along too well together. She used to say he treated her

cruel, before she stopped talking about it." There was a
queer little smile on Meyer's mouth, half anxious and half
mocking. The in-law relationship usually cut two ways.

"Cruel?"

"I don't mean he beat her, anyway not where it showed.
Mental cruelty was what she complained of. He must of
been a Tartar at that, to make her want to kill herself."

"She tried to kill herself?"

"That's right. She took a handful of sleeping-pills, way
back when they were first married. Brand tried to cover up
and pass it off as an accident, but I got the truth of it
from Annie. Annie was with them in those days."

"What made her want to do it?"

"I guess he made her life so miserable that she couldn't
stand it. I don't know. I never understood any woman, let
alone my own girls. I never could talk to either of them.
I say black, they say white—that's the way it's always
been."

His raw and broken sentimentality depressed me. The
barren little office was stifling hot, and I felt as if I'd
been trapped in it for hours.

"Where do you think she is?"

"Search me."

"You could try your house."

"Yeah," he said dubiously.

He picked up the receiver and dialed again. At the other
end of the line the telephone chirped like a tired cricket.

"Hilda? Is that you? What the hell are you doing there?
—No, hold it. I want to talk to you. And Archer has something to show you. We'll be right over."

I followed his Lincoln across town and parked in the
drive beside his private junkyard. The house was even
uglier by daylight, a peeling yellow face with blinded windows, surrounded by a wild green hair of eucalyptus
trees. If Hilda Church had traded her marriage in on this,

there was something very wrong with the marriage.

She opened the screen door for us. Meyer looked her up and down and brushed in past her without a word.

"How are you, Mr. Archer?"

"I could be better. I have been worse. And you?"

"I'm perfectly all right. Thank you." But she looked as though she had spent a bad night. Her green eyes were dusky and vague, and there were bluish patches under them. She smiled with false brightness. "Please come in."

She led me into the living-room, walking with obvious hesitancy. She reminded me of a small girl moving awkwardly in a body that had outgrown her, threatened by the sharp corners of the world.

I sat on the old davenport across from the fireplace. Its ashes had been cleaned out. The entire room had been swept and dusted and set in order. Meyer didn't seem to notice. She looked at him reproachfully, wiping her nervous white hands on her apron front.

"I've been cleaning the house for you, Father."

He answered without looking at her: "You don't have to stay here and do for me. You'll be better off in the long run if you go home and look after your husband."

"I'm not going back," she said sharply. "If you don't want me here, I'll go and find a place of my own, like Anne."

"Anne's another story. She's got no permanent ties, and she's self-supporting."

"I can support myself, too, if you don't want me."

"It isn't that. If you're set on staying here, it's okay by me. Only how's it going to look to other people?"

"What other people?"

"People in town." He gestured loosely. "All the people that voted for Brand. It doesn't make a good appearance, breaking up the family at a time like this."

"I have no family."

"You could have if you wanted to, you're not too old."

"What do you know about it?" she said in a breaking voice. "I'm not going back and that's final. It's my life."

"It's his life, too. You're fouling it up for him."

"He fouled it for himself. He can do what he wants to with his life. I don't belong to him, or anybody."

"You never talked like this before." Meyer sounded bewildered.

"Brandon never acted like this before."

"Why, what did he do?"

"I wouldn't tell you, I'd be ashamed to." Tears glazed her eyes. "You were always after Anne and me to come home and keep house for you. Now that I'm doing it, you're not satisfied. You don't like anything I do."

"Sure I do, Peaches."

He tried to touch her shoulder. She drew away. His unpracticed hand hovered in the air for a tremulous instant, then dropped to his side.

I stood up, hoping to break the weary tension that stretched between them. "Mrs. Church, I have something here for you to look at." I produced the talismanic heel. "Your father thought you might be able to identify it."

She went to one of the windows and raised the blind. Light poured in over her head and shoulders, electroplating her brown hair. She turned the leather object in her hand.

"Where did you find this?"

"In the mountains near Lake Perdida. Did your sister have a pair of walking shoes that shade of brown?"

"Yes, I think she did. In fact I know she did." She crossed the room toward me, clumsy with agitation. "Something has happened to Anne. Hasn't it? Tell me the truth."

"I wish I knew it. If that's her heel, she was out in the woods with Kerrigan last Monday, digging a hole in the ground."

"Digging her own grave, maybe," Meyer said lugubriously.

"You think she's dead, Mr. Archer."

"I don't mean to frighten you unnecessarily, but it's a good idea to expect the worst. Then any surprises we get will come as a relief."

She looked down at the heel clenched in her fist. When she opened her hand, I saw that the nails had made red indentations in her palm. She laid it against her mouth and closed her eyes. I thought for a second she was going to faint. Her body swayed slightly but heavily like a marble statue rocked on its base by an aftershock. But she didn't fall.

Her eyes opened. "Is that all? Or is there more?"

"I found these in Kerrigan's cabin at the lake." I showed her the brown bobby pins that I'd picked out of the bearskin.

"Anne always wore bobby pins like that."

Meyer peered over her shoulder. "That's right, she used to scatter them around the house. So she spent the weekend with Kerrigan, eh?"

"I doubt it. But there was a man with her. Do you have any idea who he was?"

Father and daughter looked at each other wordlessly.

"Tony Aquista was up there last Saturday night."

"What was Tony doing at the lake?" Meyer said.

"He could have been the man. They were pretty close at one time, closer than you realize."

"I don't believe it." Hilda's face was white and rigid. "My sister wouldn't touch him with a ten-foot pole."

"That's what you think," Meyer said. "You never knew what went on in Annie's head. You convinced yourself that she was a little white saint, but I know damn well what she was. She had hot—she was always a wild one.

And she played Tony along the way she played the others, until he got too rough for her."

"It isn't true." She turned to me. "You mustn't listen to Father. Anne was never wild. She was really too innocent for her own good. It never entered her head that she could get involved in—scandal."

Meyer snorted: "Innocent! She was messing around with them before she was out of pigtails, any size, any color. I caught her in this house, right here in this very room— I whaled the daylights out of her."

Hilda's face was pale and shiny, except for the dark crepe patches under her eyes. She said in a measured voice: "You're a dirty old liar."

He turned dead white. "So I'm a dirty old liar, am I?"

"Yes, and I'll tell you why. You liked her too much. You were jealous of the boys, jealous of your own daughter—"

"You're a crazy woman, talking like that in front of a stranger, blackening your old man."

His voice strangled in his throat. His hand flew up as if of its own accord and struck her once, sharply, across the face.

"Don't, Father."

I stepped between them, facing Meyer. Emotion shook him the way a terrier shakes a rag. It let go of him suddenly. He collapsed on the davenport, limp as a corpse, but breathing audibly through his mouth.

I stood over him. "Meyer, who killed your daughter?"

"I don't know," he said in a thin old voice. "You're not even sure she's dead."

"I'm sure enough. Did you kill her yourself?"

"You're way off the beam. You're as crazy as *she* is. I wouldn't hurt a hair of Annie's head."

"You did once. And I wouldn't throw words like 'crazy' around. They can boomerang."

"Who you been talking to?"

"A person who knows your background, and what you did to Anne."

He sat up unsteadily, his head lolling on his furred and wattled neck. "That was ten years ago. I was younger then, I didn't have good control of myself." His voice swayed heavily into self-pity. "It wasn't all my fault. She ran around the house without her clothes. Played up to me the same as she did to the others. It got so I couldn't keep her out of my room. I couldn't stop myself. You don't know how it was, being without a woman all those years."

"Get a crying towel, old man. Don't blubber to me. A man who did what you did would do murder."

He shook his head violently from side to side, as if it was encumbered by invisible chickens coming home to roost. "It's all over, all passed over. I never laid hands on Annie since that time."

"What about the gun you said you gave her? Was that a straight story, Meyer?"

"Sure it was. Honest to God." He crossed his chest with his finger, making the gesture seem obscene. "I gave her this old police positive that I had. She was scared of Aquista, see. If anybody killed her, it was Aquista. That stands to reason, don't it?"

"Who killed Aquista, then?"

"Not me. If you think I knocked off my own driver, you're nuts." His red-veined gaze rose to my face and hardened. "Listen, mister, I don't like this. I don't like anything about this. You're supposed to be working for me."

"I resign."

"That suits me down to the ground. Now get to hell out of my house."

I started for the door.

"Wait a minute, you owe me a hundred dollars. I want it back."

"Sue me."

He tried to get to his feet and fell back onto the davenport. His breathing was fast and loud. His limbs jerked convulsively. I looked around for Hilda.

The screen door slammed.

CHAPTER **20**:   *I went out after her, down the* veranda steps, across the uncut lawn. She looked back and saw me coming, and started to run. At the edge of the vacant lot her feet got tangled in the rank crabgrass. She fell on her knees and huddled there, her hair veiling her face, her white nape bare to some unknown fatal ax.

I lifted her to her feet and kept one arm around her to steady her. "Where are you going?"

"I don't know. I can't stay here with him. I'm afraid of him." Her breasts moved against me like wild things caught in a net. "He's an evil man, and he hates me. He's hated us both from the time we were born. I remember the day Anne was born. My mother was dying, but he was angry with her. He wanted a son. He'd be glad to see me dead, too. I was a fool to come back here."

"Why did you leave your husband, Mrs. Church?"

"He threatened me. He threatened to kill me if I set foot outside his house. But anything would be better than staying here."

She looked up at the blind house-front and across the vacant lot strewn with its rusty car-frames. Beyond it, in the street, a black sedan turned the corner and stopped at the curb, abruptly. I saw the white Stetson emerge from the driver's seat.

"Brand." Her body went soft against my side, as if its bones had dissolved in acid terror.

He came across the vacant lot, walking stiffly on long pistonlike legs. I went to meet him. We faced each other on the narrow path.

"What are you doing with my wife?"

"You'd better ask her."

"I'm asking you." His large hands were open at his sides, but they were taut and trembling. "I told you to stay away from her. I also ordered you to drop this case."

"It didn't take. I'm on it, and I'm staying."

"We'll see about that. If you think you can disregard my orders, push my deputies around, and get away with it—" His teeth bit off the sentence. "I'm giving you a choice right now. Be out of my county in one hour, or stay and face felony charges."

"The county belongs to you, eh?"

"Stick around and find out."

"This is where I came in, Church. Every time I run into you, you have a bright new plan for getting me off the case. I'm slow in the mind, but when a thing like this goes on and doesn't stop, I get a little suspicious. Just a little."

"I'm not interested in your suspicions."

"The D.A. ought to be, unless he's as sour as you are. If your whole county government is sour, I'll go higher."

He looked up at the white colloidal sky. "What makes you think you can talk to me like this?"

There was something histrionic in the question. I suspected that his will was bending under pressure, that his integrity was already broken.

"The fact that you're a phony. You know it. I know it. Your wife knows it."

A pale line framed his mouth, almost as white and

definite as a chalk line. "Are you trying to force me to kill you?"

"You haven't the stuff."

His lips stretched, uncovering his teeth, which glinted with gold souvenirs of childhood poverty. His eyes sank and darkened. I watched them for a signal. They shifted. His right shoulder dropped.

I ducked inside of his swing. His fist went by like a blundering bee, stinging my ear in flight. He staggered sideways off balance, open to a left to the jaw or a right to the middle. I let him have the right. His stomach was like a plank under his clothes. He blocked my left with his right forearm and countered with a left of his own. It caught the side of my head and whirled me around.

Hilda Church was crouched at the edge of the lot like a frightened animal. Her eyes were wide and empty, and her mouth was open in a silent scream.

I turned on Church with my face covered. His fists drove in under my elbows and doubled me over. I came up from underneath with an uppercut that turned his face to the sky. His hat fell off. He staggered backwards a few steps and went down. Rolled over and got up and came at me again.

His long left found my stomach, then my nose. Rainbowed in my streaming vision, he pivoted from the waist and brought his hooked right over. It chopped me down. I got up onto my knees and felt his fist explode in my face again. It must have opened the gash in my brow. Liquid warmth ran into one of my eyes and turned the daylight red.

I got up and went after him with my head down and bulled inside his left and hammered his body. He dropped his guard. I looped a right at his jaw, felt the pain of the impact electric to my elbow. His dazed profile turned

sideways, nimbused with red. I measured him with my left
and put my weight behind a short right hook. He went
down with his back against the side of a wheelless T-
model.

He was slow getting up this time. His feet dragged in
the withered grass. Gravity pulled at his arms. I could
have gone over his slipping guard and finished him. Instead I tied him up, partly because he was beaten and
partly because the woman cried out behind me:

"Stop it! You have to stop it!"

I held his arms immobilized. His face was like a skull
covered with stretched parchment. The scar in his temple
was red and beating. He struggled to get loose, closing
his eyes in the agony of effort. My blood ran onto him and
mixed with his, and I had my first clear thought since the
fight began. One of us was going to have to kill the other.

Fury surged through him again. He kneed me and flung
himself backwards, out of my hold. He staggered sideways
in the weeds, steadied himself on the wheelless car. There
was a frozen stillness. I saw Church leaning sleepily on
the car-frame, the trees steady in the windless heat, the
mountains behind the trees ghostly and two-dimensional
in the haze. His hand went to his hip in a jerky mechanical
motion.

Fear ran through me like a jagged spark. I had a gun
in my pocket. I didn't reach for it. That would be all he
needed to make it self-defense. And he was law.

The .45 in his hand dragged him toward me. His slouch-
ing silence was worse than any words. If I was going to
get it, this was the time and place, under a white valley
sky, in the middle of a case I'd never solve. Sweat ran in
cold runnels under my clothes, and the drip of blood from
my chin counted off the seconds.

The woman stepped around me. "Brand. This man has

been kind to me. He doesn't mean any harm. Don't hurt
him. Please."

Her hands reached for the gun and pushed it down.
She walked close into him and stood with her face against
his shoulder. "Say that you won't hurt him. Please. There
mustn't be any more killing."

He looked down at the top of her head as if he had
never seen her before. Slowly his eyes focused.

"There won't be any more." His voice was deep in his
throat. "I came to take you home, Hildie. Will you come
home with me?"

She nodded, leaning against him like a dutiful doll.

"Go and get into the car, then. I'll be along in a minute."

"No more trouble? You promise?"

"No more trouble. I promise."

He thrust the blue gun back into its holster. Their bodies
came apart gradually like a giant cell dividing. She walked
with stunned leisureliness along the path to the street.
He watched her all the way until she was in the front seat
with the door closed. Then he picked up his hat and turned
to me, brushing it on his sleeve:

"I'm willing to forget about this, if you are."

"I'm not, though."

"You're making a mistake."

"You make your mistakes and I'll make mine."

"Damn it, Archer, can't we get together?"

"Not on any terms that would suit you. I'm staying in
Las Cruces until this thing is finished. Try slapping charges
on me and I'll show you a couple of charges of my own."

"Such as?"

"Failure to do your duty. Conspiring with hoods."

"No." He reached for my arm. "You don't understand."

I stepped back out of his reach. "I understand this. I'm
trying to solve two homicides, and something is trying to

stop me. Something that looks like law and talks like law
but doesn't smell like law. Not in my nostrils. It smells
like zombie meat. A zombie that takes the public's money
and sits behind a courthouse desk pretending to be an officer."

"I've always done my duty." But he said it without
conviction. His anger had turned inward, and his cor-
roded snarl was chewing on itself.

"Did you do it last night, when that truck broke out of
the county?"

He didn't answer. He stood and looked at the ground
between us, then turned on his heel and walked toward
his car, stumbling a little. The back of his coat was split.
There was a streak of dirt on the crown of his Stetson. In
the diffused light, his body cast a faint and wavering
shadow.

CHAPTER **21**:   *I found a doctor and had eight*
stitches put in my face. The doctor seemed to take it as a
matter of course and asked no questions. When the job
was finished, though, he asked me for twenty-five dollars
in cash. He was that kind of a doctor, or I was that kind
of a patient.

When I left his office, I had a powerful impulse to climb
into my car and drive away from Las Cruces and never
come back. I couldn't think of a single solid reason for
staying. So I drove across town to the courthouse, accom-
panied by my Messianic complex.

Its towered white concrete ell was surrounded by lawns
as green as the artificial grass that undertakers use to hide
the meaning of their work. Over the front entrance a bas-
relief of blind justice faced the sun. Far above her dim

and bandaged head, the iron hands of the tower clock pointed at three thirty.

A tiled staircase led up to the District Attorney's second-floor suite. In the anteroom a heavy blonde with commissar eyes surveyed me from behind the barricades of her bosom. After taking my name and consulting her intercom, she escorted me past several doors to the D.A.'s private office. It was a large sunlit room with a minimum of furniture. A few small human touches softened its bright impersonality: the photograph of a young and pretty woman on the desk, shelves of books that weren't all law books, a pair of Don Freeman lithographs on the walls.

I've dealt with three main classes of district attorney. One is the slightly punchy, amiable type who has failed or almost failed in private practice and ended up in the courthouse, polishing apples for the people who put him there. One is the rising young lawyer who is using the office as a springboard to higher office or a richer practice. The third type, not so rare as it used to be, is the public servant who would rather live in a clean community than please a friend or get his picture in the paper.

Westmore seemed to belong in the second category. He offered me a cigarette and lit it for me, using the opportunity to study my face. His own was thin and jut-boned, ambitious-looking to the point of asceticism. It was masked with rimless spectacles and surmounted by a brush of prematurely gray hair like upright iron filings.

After placing a chair for me, he sat down behind his desk. "You're an elusive character, Mr. Archer."

"Sorry. I've had ground to cover."

"You appear to have covered it on all fours." His voice was sharp and intelligent, threaded with irony. "As a matter of fact, I was thinking seriously of having a warrant issued."

"On what charge?"

"There are several possibilities. Resisting an officer, for instance. We take a fairly dim view of that sort of thing in Las Cruces." His mouth was prim.

"You mean Church?"

"I mean Deputy Braga."

"Braga got what was coming to him. I could have taken the girl if he hadn't tackled me."

"Braga realizes that now. However, I'd stay out of dark alleys if I were you. And I wouldn't advise you to try it again, on Braga or anyone else in the sheriff's department. The one thing that's keeping you out of jail is the fact that you did report that car at the airport."

"Church gave me credit for that?"

"Naturally. The sheriff gives credit where credit is due. And the Buick was what we needed to give us a lead on Bozey."

"So Meyer told me. I take it Bozey hasn't been caught."

"Not yet. But I've had a teletype since I talked to Meyer. Bozey's rap sheet stretches from here to there." Westmore picked up a yellow flimsy from his out-basket and scanned it. "Petty theft and vandalism when he was still in grade school, repeated car theft in the next few years; carrying concealed weapons, mugging, holdup. The usual progression. Counting a year at Preston, he's spent seven of the last eleven years behind walls."

"Where does he come from?"

"The west side of Los Angeles, originally. But he's been arrested in five Western states. His last conviction was for driving a truck for a gang of bootleggers in New Mexico. He got out in July and switched his operations to the Northwest."

"Did he knock off the bank in Portland by himself?"

"So far as they know, it was a one-man job. At least he was the only one who entered the bank."

"And he walked out with twenty thousand dollars?"

"Twenty-two thousand plus. Unfortunately for him, he couldn't spend it. They had a fairly complete list of the stolen bills, and they circularized the coast and the whole Southwest. That car-purchase in Los Angeles seems to have been his only major attempt to pass any of it. He got the car all right, but the deal backfired. He had to clear out of Los Angeles with the police one jump behind him. They checked out of a Main Street hotel less than an hour before the police got there."

"The girl was with him then?"

"They were registered as man and wife. Mr. and Mrs. John Brown." A wry smile twitched at one corner of his mouth. "A highly appropriate alias, in view of what happened to the original John Brown."

"When did they leave L.A.?"

"Six weeks ago, September the 3rd. He robbed the bank in Portland on August 15. From September the 3rd till yesterday he dropped out of sight completely."

"Not quite," I said.

He gave me a keen look. "Go on, if you know something more. I've taken you into *my* confidence."

"Do you know where Lake Perdida is, Mr. Westmore?"

"I should, I have a cottage there. Why?"

"It's one of the focal points of the case. Bozey and the Summer girl hid out there for several days in early September. And Anne Meyer was last seen at the lake—"

"How does she enter the picture?"

"She's in the middle of it. I don't know what efforts are being made to trace her. If it hasn't been done, I suggest an APB."

"The sheriff issued one on her last night. We've had no response so far."

"I think you should center your search on Lake Perdida."

"You must have reasons."

"Yes." I gave him the heel, and the keys to the cabin, and went through my story again.

He listened impatiently, tapping his desk with a restless hand, as if he could feel the seconds slipping away from under his fingers. "MacGowan may be lying. Doesn't his story strike you as fantastic?"

"It's as wild as life. If he was making it up, he'd think of something more credible. Besides, I saw the hole."

"He could have dug it himself. And he has reason to lie, if he's the Summer girl's grandfather."

"MacGowan didn't even know the girl was in trouble when he told me about the gravediggers."

"He seems to have convinced you, at least."

"Question him yourself."

"I intend to. In the meantime, I want you to talk for the record."

"That's what I'm here for."

He flicked his intercom switch and asked for a court reporter. A genteel white-haired man lugged his stenotype into the room and set it up by the desk. While his racing fingers took my story down, Westmore roved the office.

The sheriff played a purely conventional role in my account. If Westmore had been a different man, I might have spoken out. But Westmore was very smooth, and I distrusted his smoothness. He had more power than the sheriff, but I couldn't be sure how he would use his power.

Halfway through my recital, he was called out of the room. He came back bright-eyed and nervous with excitement. After the stenotypist left, he told me why:

"I've been talking to the intelligence unit from Internal Revenue. I turned over Kerrigan's books to them this morning. There hasn't been time for a complete analysis, but they're certain now that he was cheating the government."

"Income-tax evasion?"

"Yes, going back several years. He made quite a lot of

money out of his bar in the late forties, money that he didn't report as income."

"Where did the money go?"

He shrugged his narrow pin-striped shoulders. "Las Vegas, Tanforan, Caliente—much more exciting than paying income tax. The year after he bought the Golden Slipper, he started keeping two sets of books. Apparently he did it with Anne Meyer's connivance. She was his secretary and bookkeeper at that time. The government has been trying for several months to get some concrete evidence against them. They tell me they were planning to call both Kerrigan and the Meyer woman before the grand jury."

"No wonder he tried to get out."

Westmore nodded solemnly. "Donald Kerrigan was at the end of his rope, financially and morally and every other way. Even his marriage was breaking up. I spoke just now to Kate Kerrigan on the telephone. He's luckier than she is, in a sense. He's out of it."

"Isn't she?"

"Not if the government presses its case. She signed his joint tax returns, of course without knowing that he had falsified them. But they could probably take everything she has left."

I thought of Kate Kerrigan, still tangled in the consequences of a wrong choice made seven years ago. "Isn't that pretty rough on her?"

"It won't happen if I can help it. Kate's a much sinned-against woman, and she's been a saint about it, an absolute saint."

I didn't argue, though saint wasn't quite the word. "I like her, too."

"I'm glad to hear you say so. She asked after you, by the way. She wants to see you when you're finished here."

"Is she at home?"

"At home, yes. One thing I didn't tell her, and I wouldn't want it passed on to her, or anyone else." He looked at me a little dubiously.

"It'll stop with me."

"Well, it ties in with your idea that the Meyer woman is central to this case. According to Kerrigan's canceled checks, he's been paying her a thousand dollars a month for the past year."

"That's a big salary for a motel manager."

"More than he ever drew from the business himself."

"Blackmail?"

"It seems to be the logical hypothesis. Hush-money of some sort, probably connected with his income-tax shenanigans. Whatever it was, it gave him a powerful motive for murdering her. Does that fit in with your ideas?"

"I'll go along with it, at least for the present."

Westmore moved to the window and stood there for a while with his back to me. When he turned, his spectacles glared in the slanting light.

"Let's assume that Kerrigan killed Anne Meyer on Monday, and disposed of her body somehow. He knew that it would be found sooner or later, and he'd be the obvious suspect. No doubt he also knew that the Revenue Bureau was getting ready to descend on his fat neck. So he decided to get out, with as much money as he could scrape together."

"And the Summer girl."

"The girl, of course. She's the catalytic agent in the reaction. She brought her two men together, Bozey and Kerrigan, and they worked out a plan to highjack a load of liquor. Bozey had twenty thousand dollars that he couldn't spend. Kerrigan had the connections that made it possible for him to order the load and set it up for Bozey. He even arranged a temporary drop at the airbase. For these various services Bozey paid him in stolen money."

"Which Kerrigan wouldn't have been able to spend either."

"Obviously Kerrigan didn't know that. They conned him. Bozey was using the girl as sucker-bait." The underworld jargon sounded queer in Westmore's Ivy League accent.

"Maybe," I said, "but she made it real for herself. She was in love with Kerrigan."

His eyebrows rose. "How do you know that?"

"From the way she talked. Also, I saw them together."

"Isn't that rather subjective evidence?"

"You can't ignore it, though. People are human. That includes the girls in Corona, and the girls who are on their way there."

"We won't argue." His face had stiffened into an official mask. He was a bureaucrat, no matter how reluctant. "She's accessory to murder in any case. We know that Bozey shot Aquista."

"Do we know it for certain?"

"I'm convinced he shot both Aquista and Kerrigan. The bullets that killed them came from the same gun. Look at Bozey's record. It's pure chance that he hadn't killed before. He was ready to kill for that load of whisky. It was better than money to him, better than the kind of money he had. There are still states in this Union where good bootleg liquor is a valuable commodity."

"New Mexico is one. The reservation Indians pay high for it."

"I'm not forgetting it. We're watching all the highways out of the state. When he tries to drive that truck across the border, we'll take him. And we'll have our case wrapped up."

"In tissue paper."

"What about tissue paper?" he snapped.

"It doesn't hold water. You said Aquista and Kerrigan were shot with the same gun."

"That's correct. Danelaw did a good job with the bullets. The Kerrigan slug was smashed by the skullbone, but there's enough of it left for positive identification. It came from the same barrel as the slug in Aquista's chest."

"What kind of a barrel?"

"A .38-caliber revolver. Danelaw thinks it was probably an old police positive."

"If your ballistics evidence is sound, it lets Bozey out. He didn't shoot Kerrigan."

"I say he did."

"Wait a minute. Consider what that means. It means he drove the truck down the highway from the airbase to the motor court, at a time when every cop in the county was looking for him. Parked his hot rig in front of the motor court and went inside and shot his partner in the crime. What motive could he have to justify the risk?"

Westmore leaned forward across the desk, resting his weight on spread fingers, in prosecutor's position. "Kerrigan's death erased a witness against him, a witness who would be dangerous as soon as he found out that his pay-off money was useless. And Kerrigan was running away with his girl."

"It doesn't stand up," I said. "Bozey had what he wanted, and he was on his way with it. He wouldn't double back for the simple satisfaction of blowing Kerrigan's head off. And if he didn't do one murder, he didn't do the other—provided Danelaw knows what he's talking about."

"I have complete confidence in Danelaw. And I say Bozey did both murders. Or else he killed Aquista, then lent his gun to the girl to use on Kerrigan."

"That's very unlikely."

"On the contrary. Those two suppositions are the only possible ones that fit the facts. There's a certain law of economy in the interpretation of evidence."

"It's false economy if you don't cover all the facts."

He gave me a narrow cross-questioner's stare. "Is there more evidence that you're cognizant of and I'm not?"

I returned his stare, as blandly as I knew how. He wasn't the kind you could get to know in an hour, or a year. I doubted that a man as jumpily brilliant as Westmore would have his well-manicured fingers in a courthouse pie. But politics made stranger bedfellows than sex.

I got up and went to the window. Outside on the lawn a gang of trusties in jail dungarees were clipping the courthouse fire-thorn. I had no desire to join them. Somewhere out of sight, a power mower droned like an insect caught in the slow amber of the afternoon.

"I gather that you have," he said at my shoulder.

"Nothing concrete."

"Let's have it. I don't have time to waste."

"Meyer told me a tale about a gun. I don't know that I believe it. The significant thing is that he brought it up himself in the first place. He may have been trying to account for the fact that it's missing."

"What sort of a gun?"

"A .38 revolver, police positive. He claims that he lent it to his daughter Anne some time last fall. That she asked him for a weapon to protect herself against Tony Aquista."

"Against Aquista?"

"That's Meyer's story. He may be lying."

"I don't understand—I thought you were working for Meyer."

"Not any more. Something came up between us that happened ten years ago. Was that before your time?"

"Hardly. I've been in practice here for nearly fifteen years."

"You probably remember the case, then. Meyer was hauled into court for mistreating his younger daughter."

"I remember," he said grimly. "The case never came to trial, however. The girl was too frightened to testify. And

I suppose Meyer did some wirepulling. The best Judge Craig could do was find his home an unfit place for minors, and take the child out of his hands."

"What's Meyer's reputation, apart from that?"

"I believe he was a rough customer in his younger days. And I've heard he made his original capital driving for Mexican rumrunners in the twenties. That *was* before my time."

"The sheriff isn't much of a picker when it comes to in-laws."

"You don't judge a man by his father-in-law," West-more said severely. "Church knew all about the old man when he married Hilda. His main idea was to get both of the girls out of Meyer's reach. He told me that himself one night, over a couple of highballs."

"There's money in the family, isn't there?"

His face hardened. "If you're fishing for what I think you are, you can reel in your line. Money wouldn't interest the sheriff. He works a sixteen-hour day for less money than I get. Church simply fell in love with Meyer's daughter and married her. He does what he thinks is right, without regard for consequences."

"I'm glad to hear it," I said, stroking the bandaged side of my face. "Is that true of his identification man, Dane-law?"

"I'm afraid I don't follow."

"Can you trust Danelaw not to twist facts, no matter where they lead?"

"Absolutely."

"Even if they lead into his own department?"

"You can't mean Brandon Church."

I was on very thin ice, and I backed away a little. "That's your inference."

Westmore's eyes glinted like nailheads, and he smiled

frostily. "Danelaw wants to be sheriff more than anything else in the world."

"Then send him over to Meyer's house. The old man has some kind of a shooting-gallery rigged up in his basement. Danelaw may find some more of those .38 slugs that he's been working with. And then again he may not."

CHAPTER 22: *Kate Kerrigan was waiting in* my car.

"I was afraid I'd miss you," she said when I opened the door. "I took a taxi down. Mr. MacGowan phoned from the powerhouse."

"For me?"

"Yes, he's on his way to my house to see you. He wasn't very specific, but I think it's something about his granddaughter. He asked me not to mention his call to anyone but you."

I got in and started the car. High school had let out. A few blocks from the courthouse, an advance guard of hotrods and jalopies stormed the streets, followed by an irregular army of boys in jeans and pretty, barelegged girls. Some of the girls were about the same age as Jo. I wondered what set her apart from them, what made the difference.

Kate changed the direction of my thoughts. "To think," she said, "that I was one of those children, less than ten years ago. The luckiest one. Father was still alive then, and I was Homecoming queen, and the captain of the football team took me to the prom. I thought that everything was going to be wonderful, all the rest of my life. Why didn't anyone tell me?"

"Nobody ever does."

"They let me live in a dream world," she said bitterly. "They let me believe that I was special, that nothing could ever touch me. You know who I thought I was? The Lady of Shalott, watching the world in a mirror. And then the mirror cracked. Or don't you know the poem?"

"I read it in high school, too."

We rode the rest of the way to her house in silence. There was no sign of MacGowan, and she asked me to come in and wait. Her living-room was chilly in spite of the daylong sun. Echoes of the quarrel I had overheard still twittered in the walls.

She flung her black hat and gloves on a chair and motioned me into another. "It's even worse than I'd thought. Did Sam Westmore tell you?"

"A little."

"Don left me with less than nothing. Sam says I may be liable for several years of unpaid income taxes. Something I didn't even know about."

"It won't happen if Westmore has his way. He's a good friend of yours, isn't he?"

"I've always believed so."

"But what if it does happen? What if they do take the rest of your property?"

"I'll be penniless."

"Is that such a terrible prospect?"

"I hardly know. I haven't begun to face it."

"Take a look at it now. What's to be so afraid of? You're young, and pretty, and smart."

Her ringless hand moved sideways in an impatient gesture. "I'm afraid I can't respond to compliments. Not today. Thank you for the good intentions, though."

"I don't see what you have to mourn for. He did you a favor by getting himself shot. Maybe he did you another favor by throwing your money away for you."

She looked at me as if she doubted my sanity. "What can you possibly mean by that?"

"You'll be getting married again—"

"Never."

"You will, though. When you do, you'll stand a better chance of finding an honest husband, not another Kerrigan. This state is crawling with easy-money boys, drones that swarm after money wherever it is. I've met a thousand of him."

"Are there so many?"

"Walk a long block in Beverly Hills or Santa Barabara or Santa Monica and you'll see two or three of them, driving their Jags and their Caddies."

"And do they all have—wives?"

"They prey on women. As long as women own three fourths of the property in this country, there will be men trying to take it away from them, and succeeding. You belong to the biggest secret sorority in the United States: the well-heeled girls who married wrong ones and lived to regret it. It's the ladies' auxiliary of the alimony fraternity."

She gave me a long dazed look. "You live in a terrible world, don't you?"

"The real world."

"How do you stand it?"

"By not investing my feelings in gold bricks. How do you?"

"I don't. That should be obvious. I'm a delicately nurtured girl"—she ironized the phrase—"who waited too long to grow up. It's hard to grow up—no wonder so few people succeed." The deep worried cleft appeared between her brows, and she said in a different tone: "Don wasn't as bad as you think. He honestly tried, part of the time at least. It wasn't entirely his fault that he couldn't handle money. I should have helped him. I could have, in all sorts

of ways. I wasn't a good wife to him. He needed more than
I was able to give him."

"He needed more than anybody could give him."

"You're full of hard sayings this afternoon."

"Sorry. I've met a lot of Kerrigans, as I said. They're
born with a vacuum where the heart should be. Or something happens to them when they're kids. Anyway, there's
nothing in them but hunger, a hungry hole you can't fill."

"Like a woman?"

She blushed, and rose in confusion and went to the big
window. After a while she said to me, or to the heedless
city: "I couldn't have done worse, could I? When I think of
what my father was—a respected man in this valley. My
grandfather founded Las Cruces College, on land he do-
nated himself. And I betrayed them. It isn't simply their
money that I've squandered. I've squandered their reputa-
tions, everything they stood for, the whole past." She
turned and looked around the arctic beautiful room. "It
hardly seems fair, it hardly seems possible, that I could
destroy so much with a single mistake."

"It's not destroyed, and neither are you. Phonies like
Kerrigan can't destroy real people and real things."

"Can't they?"

She turned her back on me again. With her bright hair
loose on her neck, she might have been a slim young girl.
It was hard to believe that she'd gone through seven years
of a bad marriage and been widowed by a gun.

I moved up close to her. "Your life isn't over, it's only
starting."

"I'm afraid you can't console me with rustic philosophy.
—No, forgive me for saying that. You've been kind to me,
right through from the beginning."

"It was easy, Katie."

"He said I wasn't a woman. I am a woman, aren't I?"

I turned her by the shoulders and held her. She gave

me her mouth. She said with her lips against my bandages:

"I'm sorry you're hurt, Lew. Please don't take any more chances."

"I won't. It's nothing."

"Am I a woman, really? Are you—attracted to me?"

I couldn't answer her question in words.

After a time, she said: "I feel like the widow of Ephesus."

"I'm full of hard sayings, and you're loaded with literary allusions. But go ahead. It's very educational."

"You're making fun of me."

"Why not?"

She pulled my head into her carved white shoulder and whispered in my ear: "Did I make you feel like a man, Lew? Did I?"

"I felt like a man before. I still do."

"You're bragging."

"All right, I'm bragging. There's nobody to hear me except you, and you don't mind."

She laughed. There were footsteps on the veranda, dragging and uneven. The doorbell chimed.

CHAPTER 23:

MacGowan had shaved off his beard. His face was folded neatly like shiny brown paper under a sedate gray hat. He had on a threadbare blue serge suit and a black tie. It had aged him to cut off his beard and put on his Sunday clothes and drive down into the valley.

"Josephine came to me after all," he said.

I stepped outside and shut the door behind me. "Is she at the lake now?"

"No, she's on her way again. She's been roaming around in the desert all day, looking for Bozey. She was pretty petered out. I tried to get her to stay with me, but she

wouldn't stay. All she wanted from me was directions how
to get to Traverse."

"Traverse?"

"That's where Bozey is, apparently. Josephine's gone to
find him."

He leaned against the doorframe, exhausted by the effort
of speaking out. I put an arm around his shoulders to steady
him. His bones were scarecrow thin.

"Did she tell you this?"

"She didn't say *he* was there; I figured that out for myself. When they were with me in September, he was very
much interested in the place—I should of thought of that
sooner, when I was talking to you. He asked me quite a few
questions about it."

"What kind of questions?"

"Where it was, and how to get there."

"And you told him?"

"I didn't see no harm in it at the time. Traverse is over
on the other side of Baker, the Nevada side. You turn off
the highway at a little hamlet called Yellow Ford, and from
there it's about ten miles up through the mountains to
Traverse. It's real deserted country."

"Are the roads passable?"

"That's what Bozey wanted to know. He said he would
like to try it some time for a camping trip. The road's passable all right—least it was the last time I was there. Most
of it is blasted from solid rock."

"Could he take a big truck up?"

"I don't see why not. The road was built to carry heavy
equipment."

"And Jo's on her way there now?"

"She must be. She got me to draw her a little map of how
to get to the place."

"Will you draw one for me?"

"Nope." He showed his yellow teeth in a grim smile.

"I'm going along with you, son. I'm not as fast on my feet as I once was, but I can still fire a gun if it comes to that."

I didn't try to talk him out of it.

When I went down to the street after saying good-by to Kate, he had brought a rifle out of the back of his A-model Ford. It was a medium-caliber sporting rifle with a telescope sight. He laid it carefully on the back seat of my car and climbed into the front.

I pressed the starter. "What decided you to come to me?"

"I believe you're a fair-minded man. You talk like one. I'm taking a chance that you'll act like one."

"I'll do my best."

I turned south at the boulevard, toward the city limits. It was twilight, and lights were coming on in the houses. The mountains lay like great veiled women against the green east. Some random stars began to nail up the edges of the evening.

MacGowan's voice came out of the thickening darkness: "Josephine's fallen among thieves. I couldn't sit by and see it happen and do nothin' about it. You should have seen her today, all sweaty and mussed, with a dirty face and that scared look in her eyes. I hardly knew her."

We stopped in Barstow for sandwiches and coffee, in Baker to check my tires. The air turned colder as night deepened. An hour or so on the far side of Baker, different mountains rose on the horizon. Above them the stars were massed now in white clusters. A few lights gleamed at their feet like bright droppings from the sky.

They slid along the flat terrain toward us. Suddenly the mountains were almost on top of us, blotting out one side of the sky.

MacGowan broke a long silence: "That's Yellow Ford now."

It was a general store, a filling station, a few frame houses and tarpaper shacks, a boarded-up real-estate booth surrounded by miles of vacant real estate. A canvas banner on the filling station announced Genuine Rattlesnakes and Other Reptiles on Display: Stop and See the Monsters of the Desert.

A man in a red plaid shirt came out of the station when I pulled up by the pumps.

"Ethyl."

He started the pump. His face was like a worn saddle ridden by circumstance. "You want to see my snakes while you're waiting? I got a diamondback close to five feet long."

"I'm looking for a different kind of animal."

"A Gila? My Gila died."

"A man." I described Bozey.

There was an extended desert pause. "I haven't seen him this week," he said finally.

"But you have seen him?"

"If it's the same young redhead. He came in here for gas a couple of times in the last month, and hung around for a while shooting the breeze."

"What was he driving?"

"Buick coupe."

MacGowan nudged me. "It's him."

"Where was he staying?"

"He didn't say. Somewhere in the hills." He waved his arm toward the mountains. "When he first turned up, he bought a sleeping-bag and a camp-stove at the store across the way. Claimed he was prospecting for uranium, but he was no prospector. He couldn't tell iron ore from copper."

He shut off the pump and leaned on the open window. His sun-faded eyes squinted through crinkled holes in his leather face. "He got me a little nervous after a time. I had a funny feeling, last time he was in, that maybe he was fixing to hold me up. He didn't, though."

"When was that?"

"Along about the middle of last week. Right after that

he vamoosed. What *was* he doing out here, anyway?"

"Hiding out."

"From the draft?"

"Could be. I heard he went through here early this morning, driving a big semi with an aluminum box. Did you happen to see him?"

"No. I don't open till eight."

"Maybe you saw a girl this evening. A pretty little brunette in an MG sports car?"

"Yeah, she went through a couple of hours ago. Didn't stop."

MacGowan leaned across me. "Is the road to Traverse open?"

"Far as I know. It hasn't snowed up there yet. Come to think of it, it must be open. A truck went up there today."

"An aluminum-painted truck?" I said.

"A *blue* truck, big blue van, looked like a furniture van. It went up about four o'clock this afternoon. In daylight you can see part of the road from here." He added as I paid him for the gas: "If you're thinking of driving up to Traverse tonight, you better watch the slides. It hasn't been cleared for a couple of years."

I thanked him and drove on.

MacGowan leaned forward in the seat as if he could will the car to go faster. "Josephine's there all right."

"She's not the only one."

CHAPTER 24:   *For the first few miles after we* left the highway, the road was fairly straight and smooth. Then it began to twist and turn on itself. Its surface was pitted with chuckholes, and I had to take it slow.

About halfway up the mountain, the wheels of my car plowed through a sand slide below a collapsing cutbank.

On the outer side of the road the ground fell away steeply into a canyon. Another slide ahead lay brown and furrowed in the headlights. I stopped the car and got out. MacGowan stayed in the front seat.

The slope of sand covered more than half the road. There were wide tread-prints in the edge of the sand: the spoor of a big truck. Examining them more closely with my flashlight, I found two sets of tire marks, one partly superimposed on the other. Both were fresh.

I stood up with my heart knocking on my ribs. Somewhere on the black heights above me a little whining sound fretted the silence. I didn't move. The sound grew in my ears. It was a car engine coming down the mountain.

Light flashed against the sky, defining a rocky buttress up ahead. I went back to my car and switched off the lights. There was no time to move it. I took out my gun and crouched behind the open front door. MacGowan reached for his rifle.

Headlights swung their long beams out over the canyon, swung back onto the road, and blazed in my eyes. The little sports car leaped around the curve. Its horn hooted. Then its brakes took hold. It swerved and skidded broadside into the sand and almost turned over. Flung out sideways over the low door, its driver fell face down in the road and lay still.

"It's Josephine," MacGowan said.

I ran to her and flashed my light on her face. Twin worms of blood crawled down her upper lip. Her eyes were fixed with shock, but she was conscious.

She tried to sit up and failed. I supported her with one arm. Her flesh was very soft, hung on an armature so frail that she seemed boneless.

"I'm hurt," she snuffled. "They hurt me way inside."

I wiped her bloody lip and saw then that her dress was

ripped to the waist. Her body was marked with bruises that weren't accounted for by the fall she had taken.

MacGowan climbed out of my car and toiled up the road toward us.

I said to the girl, with a hardness I didn't feel: "All you hustlers get hurt sooner or later. It's fair enough when you make a living hurting other people."

"I never hurt nobody in my life."

"What about Tony Aquista?"

"I didn't know about Tony. Honest, mister."

"What about Kerrigan?"

"Don was dead when I got there. I didn't shoot him."

"Who did?"

"I don't know. Neither does Bozey. I was supposed to meet him. We were going away together, him and me."

She was coming out of shock. Her eyes were beginning to move and regain their luster. A single tear left a bright track on her face.

I made a stab in the dark: "What happened to the money that Bozey gave Kerrigan?"

She didn't answer. But her head moved on my arm, involuntarily, and she glanced at the sports car from the corners of her eyes.

MacGowan said behind me: "Josie, are you all right?"

"Sure. I'm swell. Everything's great." Her pointed tongue moved over her upper lip. "Grandpa?"

I left her with him and searched the two-seater. There was a package under the boot in the space behind the driver's seat, an oblong package wrapped in newspaper and tied with dirty string. I tore it open. It was full of money, fifties and hundreds and five hundreds, all new bills. The newspaper it was wrapped in was a Portland *Oregonian,* dated last August. I rolled it up again and put it in the locked steel evidence case in the trunk of my car. Money and marijuana, the stuff that dreams are made of.

Jo was on her feet now, held in MacGowan's arms. She was mewing like a kitten, a draggled kitten in a stormy world:

"They made a circle around me. They broke open one of the cases and got drunk and took turns at me. Over and over and over." Her voice skipped up the octaves of despair.

His face was granite against her tangled hair. "I'll kill them, lass. How many of them are there?"

"Three of them. They came from Albuquerque to pick up the whisky. I should have stayed with you, Grandpa."

He frowned in puzzled grief. "Didn't your husband try to stop them?"

"Bozey isn't my husband. He would have stopped them if he could, I guess. But they took his gun before that, and beat him up."

I touched her shuddering back. "Are they still up there, Jo?"

"Yeah, they were loading the truck when I sneaked out. They've got the other truck stashed in the old fire station."

"Show me the place."

"I don't want to go back there."

"You don't want to stay here by yourself, either."

She looked at my car, then up and down the road as if its shadowed length was the years of her life, past and future. Without a word she climbed into the front seat.

I steered through the narrow space between the sports car and the drop into the canyon. MacGowan nursed his rifle on his knees. Jo sat between us, staring at nothing.

"Did you kill Kerrigan for the money?" I said.

"No. No. I went out there to meet him, and found him in his blood." Her voice was a hopeless monotone.

"Why the runout, then?"

"Because they'd think I killed him. Just like you do. But I wouldn't hurt Don Kerrigan. I adored him."

MacGowan spat into the wind.

I said: "You took the money from him."

"So I took the money. I had a right. Don was dead, he had no use for it. It was lying there on the office floor and I picked it up and took a car and went to look for Bozey. All I wanted was out."

"And twenty thousand dollars. Did Bozey tell you to get the money and join him?"

"No, nothing like that. I thought I was going away with Don. I didn't even know where Bozey was for sure."

"That's true. I told you that," MacGowan said.

She lifted her face to look at me. "Why don't you let me go? I didn't do anything wrong, except for taking the money. And it was just lying there." Her voice brightened. "Keep it yourself, why don't you? Nobody will know. Grandpa won't tell."

MacGowan let out a sound that might have been a sob, or a snort of repugnance.

I said: "The money isn't any good. Didn't you know that?"

"Come again."

"The money was hot, so hot that Bozey couldn't spend it. He took it from a bank in Portland, and they had a list of the bills. Nobody could spend it, anywhere. Or is this old stuff to you?"

"I don't believe you. Bozey wouldn't do that."

"He did, though. He was conning Kerrigan. The money was Confederate."

"You're crazy," she said hotly.

"Am I? Think about it, Jo. Would Bozey risk twenty grand on a deal like this if the twenty grand was any good to him? Nobody would."

She sat still for a while. I could feel her beside me, and

almost sense the workings of her small dark mind. Her violated personality was closing up again, hard and tight and defensive as a fist.

"If that's straight, I'm glad they beat him. He had it coming. I'm glad they cheated him out of his payoff."

We climbed toward the ridge, which rose solid black against the star-punctured sky. I nursed the laboring engine along in second, swinging from one side of the road to the other to avoid the holes and slides.

"Jo?"

"I'm still here. I haven't gone any place."

"You said last night that you were elected to flag down Aquista's truck, then something changed the plan. What was it?"

"Don didn't want me to take the risk," she said with a certain pride. "That was the main thing, anyway."

"What were the other things?"

"He did a favor for a friend of his. Then this friend of his did a favor for him."

"By stopping the truck and shooting Aquista?"

"Stopping the truck was all. Don didn't figure on any shooting. This friend of his crossed him up."

"Who was it, Jo?"

"Don didn't mention names. He said the less I knew, the better. He wanted me to be in the clear if the blueprint didn't work out."

"Was it Church? The sheriff?"

She didn't answer.

"Meyer?"

Still no answer.

"What was the favor Don did for his friend?"

"Take it up with Bozey, why don't you? He was in on it. Bozey went out in the desert with Don, Monday night."

"What were they doing out in the desert?"

"It's a long story. You wouldn't be interested."

MacGowan clucked like a hen. "Don't hold back now, honey. You ought to make a clean breast of everything."

"Make a clean breast, he says." Her laugh teetered on the shrill edge of hysteria. "I had nothing to do with it. I'm clean. All I know is what they told me."

"Who?"

"Tony, and then Don."

"What did Tony tell you Sunday night?"

"Don said I should keep quiet about it. Only I guess it doesn't matter any more, now that he's dead. What does? Tony followed Anne Meyer up to Lake Perdida on Saturday. She was in Don's cabin with some guy, and Tony was window-peeping. This doesn't make much sense. Nothing that Tony did ever made much sense. He only had about forty-eight cards in the deck."

"What did he see?"

"The usual, I guess. Beautiful music."

"Who was the man with her?"

"He didn't say. I think he was scared to tell me. The whole thing threw him, see. He was stuck on Anne Meyer, and when he looked in and her lying dead on the floor—"

"He saw her dead?"

"So he told me."

"Saturday night?"

"Sunday. He went up there again on Sunday. He peeked in the window and there she was, *kaputt*. At least that was his story to me."

"How did he know she was dead?"

"You've got me. I didn't cross-question him. I had a fast idea that maybe he killed her himself. He was nutty enough."

"Somebody's lying, Jo. Anne Meyer was alive on Monday. Your grandfather saw her with Kerrigan on Monday afternoon."

"I wasn't positive that it was her," MacGowan said.

"It must have been. That heel came off her shoe. Aquista must have been mistaken. Perhaps he only imagined that she was dead. Wasn't he pretty drunk on Sunday?"

"He was pixilated all right," Jo said, "but he didn't imagine it. Don drove up to the lake on Monday, after I told him about it, and her body was there, just like Tony said."

"Where is it now?"

"Someplace in the desert. Don put her in her car and drove it out and left it."

"Was that the favor he did for his friend?"

"I guess so. But he said he had to do it, he had to get her out of his cabin. He was afraid they'd pin the killing on him."

"Where did he leave her in the desert?"

"Search me. I wasn't there."

"But Bozey was?"

"That's right. He followed Don out to the desert and drove him back."

CHAPTER 25:

We came up over the shoulder of the mountain. The high valley below it brimmed with darkness, broken far down somewhere by a splash of light. I switched off the ignition and drove without lights or power, using the foot-brake to control our speed. The hushed car coasted down a winding grade, which straightened out and became the main street of Traverse.

I stopped at the top of the street, in front of an extinct restaurant whose windows had been smashed and boarded up. Featureless frame structures sprawled on the slopes, some of them trampled flat by the snows of past winters. Above them, piles of slag from the worked-out mines mimicked the mountains that stood all around.

About a quarter of a mile below us, at the far end of the vacant town, a great rectangular doorway belched white light. Two men moved in and out of the light, carrying boxes to the rear of a big van that stood in the street. Back and forth they walked with the weary automatism of lost souls laboring in the mines of hell.

"It's them," Jo whispered. "I don't want to go any closer."

"I wouldn't let you. How many guns do they have?"

"I think they all have guns. One of them, the one they call Faustino, has a tommygun."

"That's bad. You better go and sit in the alley. Get behind something, just in case. MacGowan, is your gun loaded?"

"Don't worry."

"How's your eye?"

"I shot a buck at four hundred yards a couple of weeks ago. If it was daylight, I think I could pick them off from here."

"Wait ten minutes, till I get down there. Then open fire. But save a couple of rounds. They'll probably try to make a break. This road is the only way out, isn't it?"

"Except for mountain goats."

"If any of them get away from me, take cover behind the car and see if you can stop them. Fire in ten minutes now."

"I got no watch."

"Count to five hundred, slow. All right?"

"Fine."

He got out of the car and lay down in the road. Jo disappeared into the alley beside the boarded-up restaurant. I walked down the hill with my gun in my hand, keeping close to the buildings. They were the shells of vanished businesses, a barbershop, an ice-cream parlor, a company

store. Their only patrons were chipmunks and coyotes,
quiet in the broken shadows. Altitude and silence rang in
my ears like quinine.

A hundred yards or so from the light, I went down on
my knees and elbows. The position brought back the
smells of cordite and flamethrowers and scorched flesh, the
green and bloody springtime of Okinawa. I crawled along
the fragmented pavement from doorway to doorway. My
time was nearly up.

The light poured from the open double doors of a frame
building on the other side of the street. There was a fire-
station sign above the door. Meyer's truck stood inside
with its headlights on and its rear doors open. The big
box was nearly empty. The two men were unloading the
last of the cases and passing them to a third man in the
blue van.

They were stripped to the waist, and sweating. One of
them was broad and dark, covered with curly black hair
on chest and back and arms. The other was tall, beak-
nosed, with vague pale eyes. I could see the blue tattoo
on his white forearm. He heaved a case into the van and
turned to his companion with a grunt:

"She was a sweet little piece. I wonder what happened
to her."

"Don't you ever get enough of it?"

Their voices were slightly blurred, their movements a
little uncertain. The dark man pushed a case into the van
and leaned against it. I rested the barrel of my revolver
on a piece of broken sidewalk and sighted along it, aim-
ing at the middle of the single black eyebrow that barred
his face.

An invisible fist rapped the side of the van. I fired before
the sound of MacGowan's shot came rattling down the
hill. One of the dark man's eyes broke like a brown agate.
He looked around at the light-splashed blackness with his

remaining eye. Ran toward me on buckling legs and went down on his knees and fell on his face, as Tony Aquista had fallen.

The tall man trotted shambling into the building. He came out much more slowly, step by step, with a Thompson sub-machinegun in his hands. It stuck out a saffron tongue at me and giggled. I fired too quickly and missed. The rapid slugs stitched the wall behind me, dropping nearer. Death chattered in my ear.

MacGowan's second and third shots echoed down the street. The tall man turned his vulture head and swung his tommygun away from me. I aimed slowly at his middle and fired twice. He took two steps backward and coughed. His gun clanked on the road. The van began to move.

He screamed above the clash of gears: "Wait for me, you dirty son—"

He snatched up the gun and ran stooped over, holding his belly together with one spread hand. He flung himself into the rear of the van as it wheeled in front of me. I emptied my gun at it. It passed over the man in the road and altered the shape of his body and fled up the street, the roar of its engine mounting higher and higher.

MacGowan's rifle spoke again, three times. It didn't stop the blue van. It passed the top of the street and climbed on toward the ridge, pushing its jumping plow of light.

Bozey came out of the firehouse as I was reloading my revolver. He walked like an old and sightless man, with his legs wide apart and his arms outstretched. His face was puffed and lacerated, his eyes swollen shut.

"Mike—Clincher—what happened?"

He stumbled over the man in the road, got down on his knees, and shook the lifeless body. "Mike? Wake up."

His fingers sensed the body's broken strangeness. He let out a single coyote howl and crawled away from it.

I walked toward him. The sound of my footsteps held

him cowed and crouching. He lisped through jagged teeth: "Who is it? I'm blind. The bastards blinded me."

I squatted beside him. "Let me look at those eyes."

He raised his blind face, whimpering. I pressed his eyelids apart with my fingers. The eyeballs were bloodshot but undamaged. He peered at me through little cracks of sight.

"Who are you?"

"We've met before. Twice."

He grunted in recognition and tried to grapple with me. But his movements were languid and boneless.

"Don't you know when you've had enough, boy?"

I twisted my hand in the scabbed fur collar of his jacket and dragged him up to his feet and went through his clothes. No gun. But my wallet was in his hip pocket and he was wearing my wristwatch. Its face was smashed. I loosened it and slipped it off over his hand. He didn't resist. The fight had gone out of him.

His long red hair fell over his ruined face like dragging wings. He blinked down at the body at his feet, surrounded by its Rorschach blot of blood. "So you got Faustino."

"He was careless."

"What about the others?"

"They got away in the van."

"You want to know where to find them? Turn me loose and I'll lead you to them."

"That won't be necessary. They'll never get back to New Mexico."

"You know who they are, eh?" He sounded disappointed.

"If they're the mob you drove for in Albuquerque."

"Yeah." He spat red toward the body. The sight of it had rekindled his confidence and made him talkative. "My mistake was going back and trying to work with creeps. I'm a heavy thief by profession. I work alone. But Faustino offered me twenty-five G's for the twelve hundred cases. And I let him suck me in." His voice trembled with righteous anger. "I ask him for my payoff—the stuff is worth close to a hundred G's in his territory—so he holds a tommygun on me and tells his cohorts to pay me off the hard way. I should have figured on a double play."

His fingers moved across the unfamiliar contours of his face. "I kind of wish you didn't knock off Faustino. I was counting on doing it myself."

"You won't be circulating. Any exterminating you do will be bedbugs in a jail cell."

"Maybe. Where's your home base, copper, in Las Cruces?"

"Los Angeles."

"State police?"

"Private."

"No kidding. Who do you work for?"

"Myself."

"That's very interesting." He leered with stupid cunning. "Maybe you and me can make a deal."

"What have you got to bargain with?"

"If I told you, I wouldn't have it. I'll tell you this. It could be a big one, bud, a once-in-a-lifetime setup. You and me could take over Las Cruces and open it up and run it for ourselves."

"Who's running it now?"

"Nobody. That's the crime of it. There's plenty of money in town, but no action. We could give them action."

"Wouldn't the local law object?"

"Leave them to me." He was carried away by psychopathic ambition. "Only I can't operate out of a cell. You take me back there and throw me in the clink, you're tossing away the hottest chance you ever had."

"A chance for what? To get conned like Kerrigan?"

That silenced him, but not for long. "Okay. So I made a patsy out of Kerrigan. He was taking off with my girl. She wanted something with more class, she said. So I should finance their honeymoon. Not me. But this is different. This is no con."

"I hear you telling me."

"Listen." He pawed my chest. "I know something nobody else knows. We can parlay it into something big, you and me together. I *like* you, see."

"Uh-huh. What's your special information?"

"Are we in business?"

"I have to know what I'm buying first. Why did the sheriff let you break out of the county last night?"

"I didn't say he let me out of the county."

"What road did you take?"

"You tell me. You know everything."

"The pass road, the one that goes up through the foothills."

His eyes were bright little knife-slits in the blue bulbs of his eyelids. "You're smart. We could get along. I like smart cookies."

"Have you got something on the sheriff, Bozey?"

"Maybe I have."

"Something that Kerrigan told you?"

"He didn't tell me nothing. I reasoned it out for myself."

"About Anne Meyer?"

"You catch on fast. They found the body, eh?"

"Not yet. Where is it, Bozey?"

"Wait a minute, not so fast. Are you and me making a deal?"

"If you want one. These are my terms: show me where the body is and I'll do my best to get you a break. You're on your way to the pillbox now, whether you know it or not. The D.A.'s got you tabbed for murder—"

"I didn't kill nobody."

"That won't help you. With your record, you're a natural to take the rap for Aquista and Kerrigan."

"Christ, I didn't even know that Kerrigan got it until Jo told me. I never got within half a mile of—what's his name, Tony Aquista?"

"Tell it to the D.A. He'll tell you different, and he can make it stick. They'll gas you for those murders if somebody doesn't step in and prevent it. Co-operate with me and I'll do my best to clear you. You're going to be in for a long stretch, but I won't let them gas you if I can help it."

He looked around anxiously at the black spiked horizon. His pipe-dream of power and money had blown away and left him naked, dwarfed by the giant world. Away off on the other side of the ridge a banshee wail of tires ended in a long, reverberating crash and an explosion, muffled by the distance. It was the sound the silence had been waiting for.

"What was that?"

"Your friends from Albuquerque. I hope."

He looked at me sharply, his broken nostrils snuffling in surprise. "You play kind of rough."

"When I have to."

"Why would you give *me* a break? Nobody ever gave me a break. How do I know you will?"

"You won't know it until it happens. It's a chance you have to take. Not much of a chance, after the ones you've been taking. It's in your own interest to help me find the body. I think whoever killed her killed the others, too."

"You may be right at that."

"Who was it, Bozey?"

"If I knew I'd tell you, wouldn't I? I'll show you where she is, though. Kerrigan left her in her car, down in a little canyon near Double Mountain."

I marched him up the slanting street. Jo was alone in the front seat of my car.

"What do you know?" Bozey said. "Family reunion."

The girl didn't look at him. An aura of sullen anger enveloped her.

"Where's your grandfather, Jo?"

"Gone up the hill. We heard a crash awhile back. Grandpa thought maybe the blue truck went off the road."

"I heard it, too."

I opened the left-hand door and urged Bozey into the seat between Jo and me. She pulled away from him.

"Do I have to ride with this? After the lousy trick he pulled on me and Don?"

"Don't be like that," he said. "He could have passed it south of the border—a guy with Kerrigan's front."

"I don't want to hear it. You're a rotten swindler. I hope they lock you up and throw away the key."

I turned up the grade. MacGowan was at the top, leaning on his rifle and breathing hard. Far down on the other side, in the deep trough of the canyon, there was a swirl of red and yellow fire.

He limped toward the car. "Looks like the end of them. They didn't see the two-seater in time, I guess."

Jo growled: "Good riddance of bad rubbish."

"You shouldn't say things like that, Josie. It don't show proper respect for human life."

"I'm human, too, aren't I? They never showed proper respect for *my* human life."

MacGowan climbed into the back, and we rolled down the long, unwinding road. The sports car was lying with its wheels in the air like a smashed mechanical beetle. Black skid-marks led to the deep-gouged edge of the road where the truck had gone over.

A thousand feet below, it was still burning brightly. Among the faint far odors of burning oil and alcohol I could smell Okinawa again.

CHAPTER **26**:   *The sky turned lime-white all* along its edges, then flared in jukebox colors. The sun appeared in my rear-view mirror like a sudden bright coin ejected from a machine. The chameleon desert mocked the sky, and the joshua trees leaned crazily into the rushing dawn.

I thought if this place had a god he was lonely and barbaric, tormented by colored memories, bored by the giant inhuman drama of starset and sunrise and sunset. I glanced at Bozey's sleeping face, swollen and discolored now like the face of a drowning victim hauled up out of black depths after many weeks. His head was on Jo's shoulder. She was awake and looking down at him.

I shoved the car's long shadow due west across the flatland, so tired that I had to exert a steady pressure of will to hold the gas pedal down. In sight of Tehachapi Pass, I shook Bozey awake and listened to his mumbled directions. The side road turned off to the left a few miles farther on. It led down into a hidden canyon, dwindling to a cattle-track.

The floor of the canyon was still in shadow. Four ragged buzzards wheeled above it. They soared away from the sound of my engine into the blue upper brilliance. Where the bed of a dry stream wound among scrub oaks at the foot of the slope, a black convertible stood.

"There she is," Bozey said.

I left him under MacGowan's gun and crossed the gravel to the abandoned car. The front of it was empty, the rear trunk locked. A bobcat had left the marks of his pads on the dusty turtleback.

I went back to my car for a pinchbar. From deep in the

grotesque mask of his face, Bozey's eyes followed me questioningly.

MacGowan put the question into words: "Isn't she in there?"

"I'm going to break open the trunk."

I broke it open, and she was in there, lying with her knees pulled up like a child in an iron womb. There was a badge of blood on the front of her sun-dress. The heel of one of her sensible brown shoes was missing.

I leaned over to look at her face. Tears gathered behind my eyes and almost blinded me. Not that she mattered to me. I'd never seen Anne Meyer except in a snapshot, laughing into the sun.

It was anger I felt, against the helplessness of the dead and my own helplessness. Overhead, the buzzards turned in wobbly circles like tipsy undertakers. The sun's insane red eye looked over the canyon's edge.

CHAPTER **27**:   *Her body lay on a rimmed table* made of stainless steel. It was ivory white except for the tips of the breasts, the hole under the left breast, the two long incisions curving down from the shoulders to a point below the breastbone.

A middle-aged pathologist named Treloar was working at a sink in the corner. He cleaned his instruments and set them on the sinkboard one by one: a scalpel and a larger knife, a bone-saw, an electric vibrator saw. They gleamed in the frosty fluorescent light.

He turned to me, peeling off his rubber gloves. "You had some questions."

"Have you recovered the bullet?"

He nodded and smiled with professional cheerfulness. "I went after it first thing. Had to use X-ray to find it. It pierced the heart and lodged between the ribs close to the spine."

"Can I have a look at it?"

"I turned it over to Danelaw an hour ago. It's definitely .38-caliber, but he has to use his comparison microscope to ascertain if it came from the same revolver."

"How long has she been dead, doctor?"

"I can give you a more precise answer when I have a chance to make some slides. Right now I'd say a week, give or take a day."

"Six days minimum?"

"Absolute minimum."

"This is Saturday. She was shot last Sunday then."

"No later than last Sunday."

"And she couldn't have been seen alive on Monday."

"Not a chance. I'm telling you the same thing I told Westmore. I'm scientifically certain, even without the slides." Professional pride sparkled behind his glasses. "I've done over forty-three hundred autopsies, here and overseas."

"I'm not questioning your competence, doctor."

"I didn't think you were. Your witness was either lying or mistaken. Westmore believes he was lying."

"Where's Westmore now?"

"In the hospital somewhere. Try the emergency room— they're sewing up your prisoner."

Treloar went back to the sink to wash his hands. I started for the door. It opened before I touched it. Displaced air moved coldly against my face, and Church came in.

He passed me without noticing me. All he saw was the woman under the light. He leaned on the foot of the table.

Treloar glanced over his shoulder. "Where have you been, Brand? We held up the p.m. as long as we thought we should."

Church paid no attention. His eyes were steady and

shining, focused on the woman. They seemed to be witnessing a revelation, looking directly into the white heat at the center of things.

"You're dead, Anne." He spoke to her as though he was addressing a dumb animal, or a child too young to talk. "You're really dead, Anne."

Treloar looked at him curiously and came forward wiping his fingers on a hospital towel. Church was unaware. He was alone with the woman, hidden in the intensity of his dream. His large hands moved and took one of her feet between them. He chafed it gently as if he could warm it back to life.

Treloar backed to the door and jerked his head at me. We went outside. The door shushed closed behind us.

He whistled softly. "I heard that he was stuck on his sister-in-law. I didn't realize he had it so bad." His smile was crooked with embarrassment. "Cigarette?"

I shook my head. Something deeper than embarrassment tied my tongue. On the other side of the metal door there were rough and broken sounds: a man's dry grief, a woman's name repeated in deaf ears.

"Excuse me," Treloar said. "I have to make a call."

He walked away quickly, his white smock flapping behind him.

CHAPTER **28**: *Westmore was leaning against* the wall beside the door of the emergency receiving-room. His face looked thinner and grayer, and his glasses were dirty. When he saw me he straightened up and squared his narrow shoulders.

"Good morning," he said with a kind of aggressive formality. "Where have you been, if I may inquire?"

"I snatched a couple of hours' sleep."

"That's more than I was able to do. I understand you've been leaving quite a trail of destruction—you and your old man of the mountain."

"It seemed to be indicated. You can't handle armed mobsters with kid gloves." But I felt more compunction than I admitted: red fire had swirled and flared through my morning dreams.

"I hate to say I told you so," he said. "But your sainted MacGowan seems to be a liar after all."

"MacGowan made an honest mistake. He never claimed to be making a positive identification of the woman. What I don't understand is how the heel got there. It came off Anne Meyer's shoe, didn't it?"

"No question about that. But it's obvious it was planted."

"MacGowan saw her lose it."

"So he claims. The chances are he planted it himself and led you to it deliberately. I'm holding him as a material witness."

"And the girl?"

"She's in the custodial ward. I'll interrogate her later. Right now I'm waiting to question Bozey. With the evidence we have, he should be ready to make a full confession."

"So the case is all wrapped up in a neat package and tied with a blue ribbon?"

"Thanks to you, yes."

"Don't thank me. I don't want any part of it as it stands."

He peered in surprise through his smeared lenses.

"I have a question for you, Mr. D.A. A hypothetical question."

He fended with his hands, half-humorously. "I'm rather leery of those. I've seen them last three and four hours in court."

"This one is short and simple, and not so very hypothetical. Say one of your colleagues in county government was fronting for hoods, or worse. What would your attitude be?"

"Negative, of course. I'd put him in jail."

"And if he ran the jail?"

"We won't beat around the bush. You mean Brandon Church."

"Yes. You should be questioning him instead of Bozey."

He laid a hard white hand on my arm. "Are you quite well, Archer? You've had a rough couple of days—"

"I don't have ideas of reference. And if you want to check my batting average, call the D.A.'s office in Los Angeles."

"I already have," he said. "They told me among other things that you've been a bit of a pistol on occasion. You make enemies. Which didn't exactly astound me."

"I make the right kind of enemies."

"That's a matter of opinion."

"Did Danelaw find anything in Meyer's basement?"

"Some slugs, which he's working on now. I'm waiting for his report. But whatever it is, you can't use it against Church. He's not responsible for anything that Meyer does or did." His eyes were hostile, and his voice metallic. "Do you have any evidence at all against Church himself?"

"Nothing you could take to a grand jury. I can't check his movements, or question him. You can."

"You expect me to crawl out on the same limb with you? You're pretty far out, you know. If somebody sawed it off, you'd have a long way to fall."

"I like it here. It gives me a bird's-eye view of your whole rotten county."

He bristled. "This county is clean, as counties go. Church and I have worked together for years to make it clean. You don't know him, or what he's done for this community."

Westmore's voice was trembling with sincerity. "Brandon Church is a genuine practical idealist. If there's one man in the valley whose character I'm sure of, he's the man."

"A man can change. Character can warp in the heat. I've been watching it happen to Church."

He looked at me anxiously. "Have you said anything to him?"

"I said it all, yesterday afternoon. He pulled his gun and nearly shot me with it. I think he would have killed me if his wife hadn't stopped him."

"You made these accusations to his face?"

I nodded.

"I'd hardly blame him for wanting to kill you. Where is he now, do you know?"

"In the post-mortem room, with his sister-in-law."

Westmore turned on his heel and walked away from me, the full length of the corridor. The metal door at the end brought him up short. He stood and looked at it for a while, and finally rapped with his fist.

The door sprang open. Church came out. Westmore said something to him which I missed. Church brushed him aside with a wide sweep of his arm and moved toward me along the corridor. His eyes were fixed on something beyond its walls, and he was grinning fiercely. He pushed out through the exit door. The roar of his engine split the morning and faded into the distance.

Westmore followed him slowly, walking with his head down as if he was butting his way through invisible obstacles. His mouth was distorted by internal pressure.

"If you could question Church, what questions would you ask him?"

"Who shot Aquista and Kerrigan and Anne Meyer."

"You're not suggesting he did?"

"I say he has guilty knowledge of those murders. He let Bozey get away with Meyer's truck last night."

"Is that what Bozey says?"

"Practically. He was afraid to come right out with it."

"Whatever he said, you can't use him to damage a man like Church."

"I saw Church on the pass road about one o'clock in the morning. He relieved the roadblock and took the post himself, which is highly unusual—"

He raised a stiff hand in a forensic gesture. "You're contradicting yourself. Church couldn't have been in two places at once. If he was on the pass road at one, he didn't shoot Kerrigan. And do you know for certain that Bozey took that route?"

"I don't know anything for certain."

"I suspected that. Bozey's obviously trying to fake some kind of an alibi."

I said: "You've got your hooks on one young professional criminal, so you're tying everything up in one heavy bundle and hanging it around his neck. I know it's standard procedure, but I don't like it. This isn't simply professional crime we're dealing with. It's a complicated case, involving a number of people, pro and amateur both."

"It's not as complicated as you're trying to make out."

"Maybe not, when we know the answers. We don't know them yet."

"I thought you regarded Church as the answer."

"Church puzzles me," I said. "I think he puzzles you, if you'd admit it. You wouldn't be defending him unless you had a reason."

"I'm not defending him. He doesn't need defense."

"Aren't you a little suspicious of him yourself? You saw his reaction to Anne Meyer's death."

"She's his sister-in-law, after all. And he's an emotional man."

"A passionate man, would you say?"

"Just what are you getting at?"

"She was more than his sister-in-law. They were lovers. Weren't they?"

He drew his fingers wearily across his forehead. "I've heard they were having an affair. But that doesn't prove anything. In fact, it makes it even less likely that he had anything to do with her death."

"It doesn't rule out passional crime. He may have shot her out of jealousy."

"You saw the grief on his face."

"I saw it. Murderers feel grief like anyone else."

"Who could he be jealous of?"

"I can think of several people. Aquista is one. He was an old follower of hers, and he was up at the lake Saturday night. It could account for what happened to Aquista. And Kerrigan's hold over Church, and Kerrigan's death."

"Church didn't kill Kerrigan, you know that."

"He may have had it done for him. There are plenty of ready guns under his orders."

Westmore said: "No," in a voice as sharp and high as a cry of pain. "I can't believe Brand would harm a living soul."

"Ask him. If he's an honest cop, or has any vestiges of honesty left, he'll tell you the truth. You might even be doing him a favor. He's carrying hell around with him now. Give him a chance to let it out before it burns him down."

"You're very sure of his guilt," Westmore said softly. "I'm not."

But he seemed to be deeply divided against himself. The artificial light reflected from the pale green hospital walls lent his face a ghostly pallor.

The light in the corridor altered suddenly. I turned to face the doctor who had failed to save Aquista. He had quietly opened the door of the emergency room.

"You can take him now, Mr. Westmore. The leaks are caulked, at any rate. You want to query him in here?"

"No. Send him out." Westmore sounded angry with the world.

Bozey came through the doorway. Between the bandages that swathed his head, his one visible eye swung wildly to the exit. The guard behind him put his hand on his holster. Bozey caught the movement and slumped into resignation.

Westmore led the procession to the morgue, and I brought up the rear.

CHAPTER **29**: *Treloar wheeled the bodies out* of their glass-doored compartments, one by one, and uncovered their faces. Aquista's was pale and gaunt, Kerrigan's fleshy and imperturbable. Anne Meyer was already old in death.

"Handsome cadavers," the doctor said. "Their organs were in beautiful shape, every one of them. It's a pity they had to die." He gave Bozey a mildly chiding look.

"What you bring me in here for?"

Westmore answered him. "To assist your memory. What's your name and age?"

Leonard Bozey. Age twenty-one. No address. No occupation. No hope.

"When did you last see this man, Donald Kerrigan?"

"Thursday night. About midnight, I guess it was."

"You guess?"

"I know. It wasn't any later."

"Where did you see him? At his motor court?"

"No. At a drive-in near there. I don't remember the name."

"The Steakburger," I said. "I witnessed the meeting."

"We'll hear from you later." Westmore turned back to Bozey: "What occurred at that meeting?"

"I don't have to answer. It's self-incineration."

Westmore smiled grimly. "Did a package of money change hands?"

"I guess so."

"What did you do then?"

"I went away."

"What were you running away from?"

"Nothing. I just went for a drive. I like night driving."

"Before you went for your joy-ride, did you take a .38-caliber revolver and shoot Kerrigan through the head with it?"

"I did not."

"Where is your gun?"

"I got no gun. It's against the law to carry one."

"And you never do anything against the law?"

"Not if I can help it. Sometimes I can't help it."

Westmore breathed deeply. "What about the truck you stole? What about the bank you robbed in Portland? Couldn't you help doing those things?"

"I never been to Portland. You mean Portland, Maine?"

"I mean Portland, Oregon."

"Is there a Portland in Oregon?"

Westmore leaned forward. In the flat bright light his profile was sharp-edged and thin, like something cut from sheet metal. "You're talking pretty flip for an ex-con with the blood of three citizens on his hands."

"I didn't kill any of them."

"Didn't you? Take a good look at them, Leonard, refresh your recollection." Westmore said to the guard: "Move him up closer."

The guard pushed Bozey forward to the head of Aquista's stretcher. The closed Latin face seemed to be haunted by its lifelong yearnings, persisting into death.

"I never saw him before."

"How could you shoot a man and steal his truck without seeing him?"

"I didn't shoot him. He wasn't in the truck, and I didn't exactly *steal* it. It was sitting here on the open highway, see. People oughtn't to leave their trucks sitting around in the open with the engine running."

"I see. This was one of those things you couldn't help. Was shooting Aquista another? Was that another one of the things you couldn't help?"

"I didn't shoot him."

"You didn't take your revolver and point it at this man's heart and pull the trigger and inflict a fatal wound on him?"

"I don't even own a revolver."

The interrogation went on for an hour. It reminded me of a fight between a young club fighter and an educated southpaw. Gradually Bozey was being worn down under the padded blows of words. After a while he had nothing left but a stubborn mulish terror. His voice was a croak, and the bandages that masked his face were stained with a reddish sweat.

I sweated with him, trying to guess the life behind his record. I had lifted cars myself when I was a kid, shared joy-rides and brawls with the lost gangs in the endless stucco maze of Los Angeles. My life had been like Bozey's up to a point. Then a whisky-smelling plain-clothes man caught me stealing a battery from the back room of a Sears Roebuck store in Long Beach. He stood me up against the wall and told me what it meant and where it led. He didn't turn me in.

I hated him for years, and never stole again.

But I remembered how it felt to be a thief. It felt like living in a room without any windows. Then it felt like living in a room without any walls. It felt as cold as death

around the heart, and after a while the heart would die
and there would be no more hope, just the fury in the
head and the fear in the bowels. Bozey. But for the grace of
an alcoholic detective sergeant, me.

There was another reason for my sense of identification
with Bozey. Westmore was using him as my whipping
boy, trying to force his answers to prove me wrong, and
not succeeding. Not quite.

CHAPTER 30:

I was grateful for the interrup-
tion when it came. Captain Danelaw opened the door and
called Westmore out. The room was perfectly quiet for
a moment after he left, the four living as still as the three
dead. Then I said:

"You're in a box, Leonard. If you don't talk now, you
may not have another chance. You'll be sniffing cyanide
before you can turn around."

"They can't frame an innocent man."

"But you're not innocent. You took the truck and we
know it. That makes you accessory to the driver's murder,
even if you didn't shoot him yourself. Your only out is to
turn state's evidence."

He thought about it. "What do you want me to say?"

"The truth. How did it happen?"

He wagged his head in melodramatic despair. "You
wouldn't believe me anyway. What's the use of telling you
what I saw?"

"Try me."

"You'll call me a liar. I waited for the truck out on the
highway. Kerrigan said it would be along around six o'-
clock. It went past me on schedule, in a breeze, rolling
along about sixty. It stopped a half a mile or so down the
road, and I followed along on foot as fast as I could."

"What stopped it?"

"There was a car there. A green Chevvy sedan. The Chevvy drove away, and that's all I saw."

"You saw it drive away from the truck?"

"Yeah. I was still a piece up the highway."

"Was Aquista in it? This man?"

"Yeah. He was sitting in the front seat. I guess it was him."

"Was he driving the Chevvy?"

"No. There was somebody else with him."

"Who was it, Bozey?"

"You won't believe me," he said. "I know it don't make sense."

"Say it anyway."

He lifted his arm and pointed to the stretcher where Anne Meyer lay. "Her. I think it was her."

"You saw that woman drive Aquista away from the truck on Thursday afternoon?"

"I told you you wouldn't believe me."

Treloar shook his head from side to side in sad tolerance. "You'll have to do better than that, boy. This woman has been dead for a week."

"You saw her body Monday night," I said.

Bozey began to talk in a high, rapid voice: "What's the use? You don't believe me when I tell you the truth. You're all a bunch of creeps." He raised his handcuffed arms and shook them at us. "You're all in cahoots with the sheriff, tryin' to railroad me and cover up for yourselves. Go ahead and gas me. I'm not afraid to die. I'm sick of breathing the same air you bastards breathe."

The guard struck him across the face with the back of his hand. "Knock off now, guy. You're getting loud."

I pushed between them. "What's that about the sheriff?"

"He was there in the pass when I broke out with the

truck. He sat there in his God-damn Mercury and let on he didn't see me—didn't even turn his head when I went by. He was setting me up for the murder rap. I can see it now."

"There won't be any murder rap if you're leveling."

"Won't there? He's got you all on a string."

"Not me. And I've cut down bigger ones."

"Who did they fall on? People like me?"

It was a hard question.

Danelaw opened the door and looked in. "What's the trouble?"

"No trouble. Is Westmore out there?"

"He left."

"Left?"

"That's right. He's got some official business."

I stepped out into the corridor. "This is a hell of a time for Westmore to leave."

"He has a hell of a reason. Meyer's waiting for him at the courthouse." He hooked his thumbs in his belt and looked complacent. "I just arrested Meyer."

"On what charge?"

"Murder. I went over to Meyer's house last night and got his permission to look around. I let on I was searching for traces of his daughter. He made no objection, probably didn't know what could be done with old bullets. There were plenty of old bullets in that shooting-gallery of his down in the basement. I dug some out of the boards where he pins the targets.

"Most of them were too beat up to be any use to me. A few were in pretty good shape, though—good enough for the comparison microscope. It took me until now to sort them out and make my case, but I made it. Some of the slugs in Meyer's basement were fired from a .38 revolver. And the ones that were good enough to compare came from the same revolver as the murder slugs. That includes the one that killed Anne Meyer."

"Are you sure?"

"I can prove it in court. Wait until you see my blown-up microphotos. I can prove it even if we never find the gun. You see, Meyer has a .38 revolver registered under his name. I asked him for it when I arrested him. He told me a cock-and-bull story, claimed he didn't have it any more."

"What was his story?"

"He said he lent it to his daughter last fall and never got it back. Of course he's lying."

"I thought so yesterday. Now I'm not so certain."

"Sure he's lying. He has to lie. He's got no alibi for any of the shootings. He was by himself all day Sunday, when Annie got it, and he had plenty of chance to drive up to the lake. On Thursday afternoon, he claims his other daughter for an alibi. But she was right there in his house from five o'clock on, and he didn't get home until after seven. He admits that himself, he claims he went for a drive when he left the yard. The same for the Kerrigan shooting. No alibi."

"No motive, either."

"He had a motive. Aquista and Kerrigan both went with Annie at one time or another." His thin nose wrinkled, as if it detected an odor worse than iodoform. "And Meyer had some kind of an insane crush on his own daughter."

"It's a pretty story," I said. "Did you tell it to the sheriff?"

For the first time Danelaw seemed uneasy. "I haven't seen him. Anyway, I wouldn't want to put him in the position of arresting his own father-in-law. I went over his head for once and laid it out for Westmore."

"And Westmore bought it?"

"Sure he did. Don't you?"

"I'll take an option on it. But I want to do a little more shopping around. Meyer drives a Lincoln, doesn't he?"

"That's right. He has another car, too, an old Chevvy he uses for transportation."

"A green Chevvy sedan?"

"Yeah. I'm going to work on those cars next shot out of the box. One of them must have been seen around the time and place of one of the shootings."

"I can save you some trouble there. Talk to the prisoner inside. Ask him about the car Aquista drove away in on Thursday."

Danelaw turned to the door. I went the other way.

CHAPTER 31: *Hilda Church opened the front* door and looked out shyly. In her quilted cotton housedress she might have been any pretty suburban chatelaine interrupted at her morning work. But there was a tight glazed look around her eyes and mouth. Her eyes were translucent and strange, a clear pale green like deep ocean water.

"Is your husband home, Mrs. Church?"

"No. I'm afraid he isn't."

"I'll wait."

"But I don't know when he'll be back."

"It doesn't matter. I have things to discuss with you."

"I'm sorry, I don't feel like talking to anyone. Not this morning."

She tried to close the door. I held it open.

"You better let me come in."

"No. Please. Brandon will be angry if he comes home and finds you." She leaned her weight on the door. One side of her breast bulged around its edge. "Please let me close it. And go away. I'll tell Brandon you called."

"I'm coming in, Mrs. Church."

I set my shoulder against the door and forced it open. She retreated to the doorway of the living-room and stood in it, her arms stiff at her sides, her fingers working at the ends of them. She looked sideways at me, with a kind of fearful coquetry. The cord in the side of her neck was strung taut like a thin rope.

I moved toward her. She retreated farther, into the living-room. She walked with a queer cumbersomeness, as if her body was lagging far behind her thought. Stopping beside a bleached mahogany coffee table, she leaned over and moved a white clay ashtray a fraction of an inch, into the table's mathematical center.

The ashtray, the table, the rug, everything in the room was clean. The white and black-iron furniture was bleakly new, and geometrically placed around the room. Through sliding glass doors I could see out into a white-walled patio blazing like an open furnace with flowers. A circular brick planter overflowed with masses of purple lobelia, in the middle of which a dwarf lemon tree held its wax blossoms up to the sun.

"What do you want with me?" she whispered.

The light reflected from the patio wall fell stark across her half-averted face. She looked so much like the dead woman in that instant that I couldn't believe in her reality. Death had aged Anne Meyer and made them almost twins. Time jarred to a stop and reversed itself. The helpless pity I had felt for Anne went through me like a drug. Now I pitied the unreal woman who was standing with her head bowed over her immaculate coffee table.

She had acted beyond her power to imagine what she had done. I had to drive the truth home to her, give her back reality, and regain it for myself. I'd rather have shot her through the head.

"You killed your sister with your father's gun. Do you want to talk about it now, Mrs. Church?"

She looked up at me. Through her tide-green eyes I could see the thoughts shifting across her mind like the shadows of unknown creatures. She said: "I loved my sister. I didn't mean, I didn't intend—"

"But you did."

"It was an accident. The gun did. The gun went off in my hand. Anne looked at me. She didn't say a word. She fell on the floor."

"Why did you shoot her if you loved her?"

"It was Anne's fault. She oughtn't to have gone with him. I know how you men are, you're like animals, you can't help yourselves. The woman can help it, though. She shouldn't have let him. She shouldn't have led him on.

"I've done a great deal of thinking about it," she said. "I've done nothing but think about it since it happened. I haven't even taken time to sleep. I've spent the whole week thinking and cleaning house. I cleaned this house and then I cleaned father's house and then I came back here and cleaned this house again. I can't seem to get it clean, but I did decide one thing, that it was Anne's fault. You can't blame Fath—you can't blame Brandon for it, he's a man."

"I don't understand how it happened, Mrs. Church. Do you remember?"

"Not very well. I've been thinking so much. My mind has been working so quickly, I haven't had time to remember."

"Did it happen on Sunday?"

"Sunday morning, early, at the lake. I went there to talk to Anne. All I intended to do was talk to her. She was always so thoughtless, she didn't realize what she'd done to me. She needed someone to bring her to her senses. I couldn't let it go on the way it had. I had to do *something*."

"You knew about it then?"

"I'd known for months. I saw how Brand looked at her, and how she acted. He'd be sitting in his chair and she'd walk close to him so her skirt would brush his knee. And then they started to go on weekend trips. Last Saturday they did it again. Brand said that he had a meeting in Los Angeles. I called the hotel and he wasn't in Los Angeles. He was with Anne. I knew that, I didn't know where.

"Then Tony Aquista came here Saturday night. It was very late, past midnight. He got me out of bed. I wasn't asleep, though. I was thinking already, even before it happened. When he came to the door and told me, I could see everything all at once, my whole life in a single instant—the city and the mountains and the two of them in the cabin with each other, and me by myself, all by myself down here."

She raised her hands to her breasts and gripped them cruelly.

"Go on," I said. "What did Aquista tell you?"

"He said that he followed her to Lake Perdida and saw her with Brand. He said that they were on the bearskin rug in front of the fireplace. The fire was burning and they had no clothes on. He said that she was laughing and calling out his name.

"Tony was drunk, and he hated Brand, but he was telling the truth. I knew he was telling the truth. I sat all night after he left, trying to think what to do. The night went by like no time at all. And then the church bells started ringing for early Mass. They came as a sign to me, they sounded like my own wedding bells, and all the way driving up to the lake they kept on ringing. All the time I was talking to Anne, they were ringing in my ears. I had to shout so I could hear myself. They didn't stop until the gun went off."

She shuddered, as if she could feel its fiery orgasm penetrating her own flesh.

"Where was your husband when it happened?"

"He wasn't there. He left before I got there."

"Where did you get the gun? From your father?"

"It was Father's revolver. But he didn't give it to me. Anne did."

"Your sister gave it to you?"

"Yes." She nodded her fine small head, birdlike. "She must have. I know she had it. And then it was in my hand."

"Why would she do that?"

"I don't know. Honestly. I can't remember." Her face went completely blank. "I try to think back and it's just a blur with Anne's face in it, and the sound of the bells. Everything moves so fast, and I'm so slow. The gun went off and I was terrified, there by myself with her body. I thought for a minute that it was me, lying dead on the floor. I ran away."

"But you went back?"

"Yes. I did. On Monday. I wanted to—to give Anne decent burial. I believed if I could bury her I wouldn't have to be thinking constantly of her lying there."

"Was Kerrigan there at the lodge? Or did he walk in on you and find you with her body?"

"Yes, he came when I was there. I was trying to drag— to carry her out to her car. Mr. Kerrigan offered to help me. He said he couldn't afford to leave her there, that he'd be suspected of shooting her himself. He drove me to a place where I could bury her, in the woods. Then that awful old man came spying on us." Anger darkened her eyes, fleeting and meaningless as a child's anger. "It was the old man's fault that I couldn't give my sister decent burial. He made me fall and hurt my knee."

"And lose your heel?"

"Yes. How did you know? Anne and I wear the same

size and style of shoe, and Mr. Kerrigan said if I changed shoes with her, no one would ever know the difference. I left *her* shoes at her apartment when we went to destroy the evidence."

"What evidence?"

"Mr. Kerrigan didn't tell me. He just said that there was evidence against me in Anne's apartment."

"More likely evidence against him. Your sister was blackmailing him."

"No, you must be mistaken." Her tone was both defensive and superior. "Anne was incapable of anything like that. She was thoughtless, but she wasn't consciously evil. She didn't mean to be bad."

"Nobody ever does, Mrs. Church. It creeps up on people."

"No. You don't understand. Mr. Kerrigan was helping me. He said it wasn't fair that I should have to suffer for Anne—for Anne's mistake. She was in the trunk of her car, and he offered to drive it out and leave it where it wouldn't be found, not for a long time."

"And what did he want from you, in return for all his help? Another accident?"

"I don't remember." But her look was evasive.

"I'll remember for you," I said. "Kerrigan told you to be out on the highway Thursday afternoon along toward evening. You were to stop Aquista's truck and get him out of it somehow. You went to your father's house, partly to get an alibi started, and partly to borrow his old Chevvy. Why did it have to be your father's car?"

"Mr. Kerrigan said that Tony would be certain to recognize it."

"He thought of everything, didn't he? Nearly everything. But he didn't know that you had a reason to kill Aquista. Or did he?"

"What reason? I don't understand."

"Aquista could figure out, if he hadn't already, that you had murdered your sister."

"Please don't use that word." She looked up wildly, as if I had released something fearful and blind in the room, a bat that might dive and cling to her hair. "You mustn't use that word."

"It's the correct word, Mrs. Church. For all three shootings. You murdered Aquista in order to silence him. You pushed him into the ditch and drove back to your father's house to complete your alibi. That left one witness against you—Kerrigan."

"You make it sound so evil," she said, "so planned. It wasn't that way at all. When Tony got into the car, I told him the first thing that came into my head: that Father had had an accident. I didn't intend to shoot Tony. But he saw the gun on the seat and it made him suspicious. He made a grab for it. I had to pick it up before he got it, I didn't trust him. Then I couldn't drive and watch him and hold the gun all at the same time. He grabbed for it again."

"And it went off again?"

"Yes. He slumped down in the seat and began to breathe queerly." Her shoulders sagged in unconscious mimicry, and her breath rustled in her throat. "I couldn't stand the sound of him, the sight of the blood. So I put him out of the car." She thrust her arms out violently, against thin air.

"The gun went off once more," I said. "Do you remember the third time? In Kerrigan's office?"

"Yes. I remember." Her voice was firmer, her look more definite. It seemed to have strengthened her, in some secret way, to re-enact her murders and confess. "The others were accidents—I know you don't believe me. But I killed Mr. Kerrigan because I had to. He had told Brand about the others. Everything. I had to prevent him from telling other people. Brand locked me in that night, but then he had to go out again. I broke a window and went to the motor court. Mr. Kerrigan was in his office, and I walked in and shot him. I hated to do it, after all the help he gave me. But I had to."

I looked into the shadowed depths of her eyes, unable to tell if the irony was intended. She was as stern and unsmiling as a judge with his black cap on.

"Three killings with three shots is quite a record. Where did you learn to shoot so well?"

"Father taught me, and Brandon used to take me out on the range. I sometimes scored a hundred in silhouette."

"Where is the gun you used?"

"Brandon has it. He found it where I hid it. I'm glad he found it."

I looked at her questioningly.

"I don't want anything more to happen," she said. "I hate killing and violence. I always have. I couldn't even bury a dead cat when I was a girl, or take a mouse out of a trap. While I had the gun, I had no peace."

"Neither did anyone else."

She didn't hear me. Her face had the look I had seen on it Thursday night, both frightened and expectant. A car stopped in the drive.

32

CHAPTER **32**:   *I waited for Church with my* gun out. He came into the doorway, bright-eyed and haggard under his Stetson. His hand went into the side pocket of his suit coat, which bulged with the shape of a gun.

"I thought that you would be the one," he said.

"You should have shot me when you had the chance. I wouldn't try it now, though. Your wife here scored a hundred in silhouette. I used to score ninety-nine in rapid fire."

"I'm not competing, Archer. I don't want your blood on my hands."

"Let me see your hands."

He held them out in front of him, palms up and empty. He winced when I took the gun out of his pocket. It was a blue steel revolver, a .38-caliber. The butt was suave from use. I twirled the well-oiled cylinder. It was fully loaded.

"Take it," he said. "It's the one you want."

He looked from the gun to the woman. She had backed against the glass door to the patio. Her eyes were terrible green gashes in her still face. They overflowed, and I wondered who her grief was for. Herself?

"You told him, Hilda?"

She nodded dumbly.

He said to me: "You know, then."

"Yes. Where have you been?"

"Out on the highway. I had a childish kind of idea that I could go away and leave it all behind, start over somewhere else."

"So here you are."

"Here I am. I realized that I couldn't leave myself behind, that I'd have to go on living with myself no matter where I was. A cheerful prospect." He was trying to be sardonic, to hold a style, but his raw pain showed through. "There's more to it than that, of course. I couldn't go away and leave Hilda to face these things alone. I'm guiltier than she is."

She moaned. Her face was like a statue's in the rain. "Brandon, let me go outside. Please? I can't stand to hear you talk like that."

"You won't run away?"

"I promise."

"You won't hurt yourself?"

"No, Brandon."

"All right. For a little while." He turned to me as the glass door slid closed behind her. "She won't leave the patio, don't worry. She loves it there, and she hasn't much time."

"You still care for her?"

"She's my child. That's the hell of it, Archer. I can't blame her, she's not responsible. I'm the one who's responsible. She acted under inner compulsion, hardly knowing what she was doing. I knew damn well what I was doing, right from the beginning. I went ahead and did it anyway. This is the payoff."

He opened his large hands and looked down into them. "It really came Thursday night, when Kerrigan told me what she had done. He let out a few snide hints when we were at the motor court. I went to his house later, and he threw the whole thing at me. It was the first I knew of it. It was the first I knew that Anne was dead.

"I'm not making excuses for what I did. I don't believe I would have done it, though, if I'd been thinking straight. He gave me a bad shock. I wasn't prepared for it. The last I saw of Anne, you see, it was a sunny morning up at the lake, and we were happier than we'd ever been." Bright droplets pimpled his forehead. He brushed at them impatiently. "God damn it, I'm falling into self-pity. It's my vice.

"But it was like going through an earthquake that night at Kerrigan's house. My whole life tilted up and fell on me. My girl was dead. My wife had killed her, and then she'd killed again. Kerrigan didn't spare me anything, he said whatever he could think of to break my resistance. I didn't really believe him until I questioned Hilda. But she admitted everything—everything she remembered.

"I couldn't see any way out that night. I still can't. I went out to the pass road and did what Kerrigan wanted me to do. You had it right, Archer." The words came painfully from his grim mouth. "I relieved my men and let the heister go through, out of my county. It's the thing I'm most ashamed of, out of all the things I have to be ashamed of."

"He's back in your county again."

"I know. It doesn't alter what I've done."

I was embarrassed by the guns in my fists. I shoved them down into my jacket pockets, out of sight. My judgment of Church had been turned upside down in the last few minutes. He had broken some of the rules. His life had been disordered and passionate. But he was an honest man according to his lights.

"I'd have done the same," I said.

"You're not a sworn officer. And aren't you changing your tune?"

"I was wrong yesterday. I retract what I said. Forget it."

"I can't forget the truth. I've been running around the countryside for the last forty hours pretending to enforce the law. Actually, I was looking for Anne. Kerrigan wouldn't tell me where she was, it was another hold he had on me. Well, it's over now. I suppose Westmore will be asking the grand jury for a formal accusation against me."

"Not if I can help it. And I'm his main witness."

He looked at me in surprise. "After what I've done?"

"After what you've done."

"You're an unusual man," he said slowly.

"Double it. You're the sort of conscience-stricken bastard who would get satisfaction out of public disgrace and maybe a term in your own jail. Naturally you feel guilty. You are guilty. You made some bad mistakes. The worst one you made was leaving Hilda at large after you knew that she'd committed murder. Kerrigan was no loss to anybody, but it might have been somebody else."

"I know I shouldn't have left her that night. Kerrigan forced me to: he made me go out to the pass. I should have taken her to the psychopathic ward. But I couldn't then. My own mind wasn't clear. I felt so wrong myself."

His gaze moved past me to the glass door. Hilda was standing idly in the patio, staring at the white-flowered lemon tree. She seemed lost, as if she had wandered into someone else's garden by mistake. Church made an inarticulate noise. He took off his hat and threw it at the wall and sat in an iron chair with his head in his hands. I sat down across from him.

When he uncovered his face, his eyes were not so feverishly bright. The lines in his face were deeper. His hands were shaking. He clasped them to hold them still, in a prayerful attitude. In spite of his rumpled business suit, he looked like a ravaged saint stretched on El Greco's rack.

"Hilda's going to spend a long time behind walls," I said. "The place depends on whether or not she's sane. Is she insane?"

"I don't know what a jury will say. She's emotionally disturbed, you can see that for yourself. She's never been entirely normal since I've known her. It's one of the reasons I married her, I think. Her life at home with Meyer was driving her insane, literally. Some men have a need to be needed. I'm one of them.

"I know now it's more of a weakness than a strength, not a good basis for a marriage. It worked, though, for nearly ten years. If we could have had children, it might have worked permanently. Or if I hadn't lost my will." His eyes were on me, but they didn't see me. He was deep inside of himself, probing for the truth he had to live by. "I think will is just another name for desire. In the long run you can't force yourself to will what you don't desire. Or stay away from the things you really want.

"I wanted a son," he said in a deeper voice. "She couldn't give me one. The son I couldn't have, all the other things I was missing out of life—they gradually wore me down. Our life together was empty. We tried to fill it with things, a new house, furniture"—he looked around the barren sunlit room—"but there was no fun in it. No love. I didn't love Hilda any more, and I don't think she ever loved me. She had too much fear in her heart to be able to love."

"What was she so afraid of?"

"It started with her father, I think, and then it spread to other things, including me. And herself." He breathed deeply. "Sometimes it was like a wild animal inside of her looking out through her eyes—an animal I had to keep fed and tamed. So long as I could give her love, the security she needed, she was safe. For nine years I kept her living along like a fairly normal person. Then I failed her. I was the one who failed. I'd overestimated my strength, and taken on too much. And I gave in."

He struck his long thigh with the edge of his hand. He seemed to be chopping his life into segments.

"I suppose I was attracted to Anne the first time I saw her. I didn't let myself know it when she was living with us, or for a long time after. She was so young, and I wasn't going to repeat what her father had done. She was like a daughter to me—a prodigal daughter when she grew up. I was too much of a Puritan to approve of Anne. But she stood for the things I'd been missing: fun and laughter and love without tears. She was so much like Hilda, yet so different—heads and tails of the same coin.

"I started dreaming about her last year, last spring when the hills were turning green. The rutting season." He was ironizing himself like an old man recalling his hot extinguished youth. But there was a lift in his voice. "I would make elaborate plans to meet her on the street, or think of reasons for Hilda to have her over. Then when she came I was afraid to go near her. She was so lovely.

"I could have stopped it. I could have stopped myself. But I was carried away by—whatever you want to call it, love, or rut, or self-indulgence. I thought I deserved more than I was getting. Well, I got more. We all did.

"In June the three of us went to the ocean for the weekend. I didn't want to take Anne along—I was fighting it at the time, and I knew I was losing, but Hilda insisted. She had some idea of getting Anne away from Kerrigan, I think. The first night we were there, Hilda had a migraine. Anne and I left her in the motel and went for a walk on the beach. We hadn't been alone together for years, not since she'd grown up, not in a private place. It happened to us."

I heard a tearing noise in the patio. I got up and went to the door. Hilda was down on her knees, ripping at the crabgrass that grew in long strands around the edge of the brick planter.

"That was my crime," Church said to my back, insistently. "I took away my love from Hilda and gave it to her sister. Anne fell in love with me, too. It got so that we had to be together, any way we could, anywhere. I'd go away for a night with Anne, and Hilda would be waiting for me when I came home with that wounded-animal look in her eyes. She never said a word about Anne, never asked me a question. She was withdrawing into herself again, the way she was when I married her. And I let it happen. I think I must have wanted it to happen. There were times when I willed her to lose her mind completely, so that I'd be free to live with Anne, to marry her and have children." His voice broke. "I got my wish, in a way."

"Has she ever been hospitalized?"

"Once, in the first year of our marriage. She tried to commit suicide. They held her for observation at the county hospital for ten days. She was going to have a baby, and the doctors blamed it on her pregnancy. She told me she didn't want to bring a child into this world. The same night she took an overdose of sleeping-pills. I got her to a stomach pump in time.

"I could have had her committed then. The doctors left it up to me. I decided to keep her at home. I believed I could give her a better life at home. And she was carrying my child."

"What happened to the child?"

"She lost it anyway. Her mental condition improved after that."

"Has she been having psychiatric treatment?"

"Some, off and on. Supportive treatment."

"Well, it's a fair background for a not-guilty-by-reason-of-insanity plea. Did she plan to kill Anne ahead of time, do you know?"

"I know it wasn't premeditated. It was done on the spur of the moment. I can prove it, if they'll take my word for it. She didn't have the gun when she went up there."

"So she told me. I didn't know if she was telling the truth."

"She was. She must have taken it from Anne, or found it in the cabin. I saw it on the bureau Saturday night, and I warned Anne about leaving a loaded gun lying around. But she wouldn't let me unload it. She wanted it for protection."

"Against Hilda?"

"That I doubt. She was never afraid of Hilda."

"She should have been. According to Hilda, Anne gave her the gun. Does that make any sense to you?"

"She told me that, too. But Anne wouldn't do that."

"I wonder. She knew that Hilda had attempted suicide."

I moved to the door. Hilda was on her knees among the flowers, but she was no longer weeding. She was tearing up the trailing lobelia in great colored handfuls and flinging them behind her. The planter looked half-scalped.

Church brushed past me and stepped down into the patio. "Hilda! What are you doing?"

She rose on her knees and glanced up at us over her shoulder. Her face was flushed and wet. "I don't like these. They're not pretty any more." She saw the shocked look on his face and cringed away from it. "Is it all right, Father, I mean Brandon?"

He answered after a breathing pause: "It's all right, Hilda. Do what you want to with the flowers. They're yours."

"I'd like to ask you a question," I said. "About Anne."

She got to her feet, pushing her hair back with a soiled hand. "But I told you about Anne. It was an accident. I had the gun in my hand and it went off and she looked at me. She looked at me and fell over on the floor."

"How did the gun get into your hand?"

"Anne gave it to me," she said. "I told you that."

"Why did she give it to you? Did she say anything? Do you remember?"

"I remember something. It doesn't seem right."

"What was said, Mrs. Church? Try hard to remember."

"She laughed at me. I said if she didn't leave Father alone that I would kill myself."

"Leave your father alone?"

"No." Her eyes were puzzled. "Brandon. Leave Brandon alone. She laughed and went into the bedroom and got the revolver and handed it to me. 'Go ahead and kill yourself,' she said. 'Here's your chance, the gun is loaded. Kill yourself,' she said." She paused, in a listening attitude. "But I didn't. I killed her."

Church groaned behind me. I turned. He looked like a man who had barely survived a long illness. A humming-bird whizzed over his head like an iridescent bullet. He watched it out of sight, peering into the blue depths of the sky.

His wife was back among the flowers, ripping the last of them out of the moist earth. When the police car arrived, the planter was denuded and she had begun to strip the thorny lemon tree. Church washed and bandaged her bleeding hands before they took her away.

THE LEW ARCHER NOVELS
BY ROSS MACDONALD

"The American private eye, immortalized by Hammett, refined by Chandler, brought to its zenith by Macdonald."
—*The New York Times Book Review*

THE DROWNING POOL

When a millionaire matriarch is found floating face down in the family pool, the prime suspects are her good-for-nothing son and his seductive teenage daughter. Lew Archer takes this case in the L.A. suburbs and encounters a moral wasteland of corporate greed and family hatred.

Crime Fiction/0-679-76806-8

THE FAR SIDE OF THE DOLLAR

Archer is looking for an unstable rich kid who has run away from an exclusive reform school—and into the arms of kidnappers. Why are his desperate parents so loath to give Archer the information he needs? And why do all trails lead to a derelict Hollywood hotel where starlets and sailors once rubbed elbows with two-bit grifters?

Crime Fiction/0-679-76865-3

THE UNDERGROUND MAN

As a mysterious fire rages through the hills of a privileged town in Southern California, Archer tracks a missing child who may be the pawn in a marital struggle or the victim of a bizarre kidnapping.

Crime Fiction/0-679-76808-4

ALSO AVAILABLE:

Black Money, 0-679-76810-6
The Chill, 0-679-76807-6
The Galton Case, 0-679-76864-5
The Goodbye Look, 0-375-70865-0
The Moving Target, 0-375-70146-X
Sleeping Beauty, 0-375-70866-9
The Wycherly Woman, 0-375-70144-3
The Zebra-Striped Hearse, 0-375-70145-1